MASTER
OF
THE
LASH

by

FORD BOWNE

On the range in the old West, where violence was as commonplace as three squares a day and as regular as the setting of the sun, some men used guns, some fists and some knives. Unlike these, Heinz used a bull-whip with such relish and such skill that he was known as the Master of the Lash, and when he fought blood ran like rain.

MASTER OF THE LASH

MASTER OF THE ___

MASTER OF THE LASH

by

FORD BOWNE

LENOX HILL PRESS

1974

6

Printed in the United States of America

11/95   Gift

MASTER OF THE LASH

1

Save for the two tired men who had prepared a late meal, the arroyo was as bare as sun-bleached bones. Sudbury Pinkham was hunkered near a small campfire, gnawing meat from the thigh bone of an unlucky rabbit.

"Tough as rawhide," he grumbled. "This jack spent most of his life running from something. Either that, or you don't know how to cook."

Pinkham was Pink, Pinky, Pink Ham, et cetera, according to Joe Enright's fancy, which at the moment came forth with a title befitting their reason for being where they were.

"Trouble with you, Pinkerton, is that you're spoiled by town living. It has softened your teeth."

"When it comes to jaw-boning rabbit, give me a nice juicy steak."

"Next time you do the hunting, aim at something bigger, like an elk or a grizzly bear. You must have scared the jack to death. You couldn't hit anything smaller than an elephant."

"Not many of them around. Did you ever see an elephant?"

Pinkham's partner and favorite disputant sat across from him, shoulder blades against a basalt slab, sipping scalding Arbuckles from a tin cup.

"Yeah. I went elephant huntin' once with a bucket."

"Catch any?"

"Another kid told me if I helped water the elephants, I'd get a free pass to the circus. They didn't have any elephants."

"Then how did you see one?"

"Not how; where. I see just like you do, only clearer. I saw one at another circus that had elephants. Man, a steak sure would taste good!"

"You gonna eat your share of this jack, or do I throw it out?"

"No hurry. I got all night. Watchin' you eat has slowed down my appetite. Pink, I had just about worked myself up to good health again after the last time you almost got me killed. I was gettin' ready to enjoy life. Then, by ding, you had to show up again. If I counted the times you've got me into trouble, I'd have to take off my boots and use my toes."

"Ho! When I rode into the ranch, your face lit up like a smoke-blacked chimney. Made you almost good-looking. I claim I did pretty good, because not even the Lord could do much about your looks."

They sat grinning at each other. Enright thrust out a knife to spear a piece of rabbit. "This is the kind of palaver I have to put up with on account of bein' prettier than most folks. Even the ones who pretend to be my friends are jealous."

The fire had burned to coals, rosy red between flat stones. Away from it, up the arroyo, their bed-rolls had been spread out near two saddles. The geldings and a pack-mare were staked out on a fair stand of bunch-grass a thousand yards down-grade near a creek pool. Nothing grew in the arroyo except occasional tufts of thistle. Higher up, gray sage and brownish juniper battled for ground room to live.

"Last time we spent together, we did have a mite of trouble," Pinkham acknowledged belatedly. "But you didn't come anywhere near getting killed. And when we parted company, you were as healthy as a frisky bull knee-deep in heifers."

"Well, you keep tryin' to get me killed. One of these days you'll make it. I hope I'm not around."

Pinkham had turned his head to look down toward the creek.

"Do you hear what I hear?"

He had finished his share of the meal, wiped his hands on the pot rag and poured a mouth rinse from the lidless coffeepot.

"I'm no deafer now than you were ten years ago. Fellow comin' this way playin' a mouth harp. What's the tune, if you know any tunes?"

Both men had risen to look toward the creek.

"Sounds like Old Dan Whosis. Maybe he wants us

to know he is coming. There he is. One man on a black horse. Can you see that far with your aging eyes?"

"That's a good horse under him. Not as good as mine, but better than yours."

"If your nag is so good, why do you keep trying to trade for mine? He is looking over our livestock."

"Now he has spotted us."

"Already had before we saw him. That's why he is playing."

"My, you're awful smart. It's a wonder your neck can hold up your head. How come you're willin' to associate with an ignoramus like me?"

"Sometimes it's hard, but I'm a charitable fellow."

"Crawlin' crawdads! That man is a mile tall and a yard across. No wonder he rides a big horse."

The rider whacked the mouth harp against the palm of his hand to free it of moisture and thrust it into the pocket of a flapping vest. He was clad in black, from his flat drover's hat to boots scuffed and scarred by rough service. The boot feet were long, his hands were long, his face like the rest of him.

"Long-beaked, too," Pinkham observed in a low voice. "Howdy, mister. Was that serenade for us? If so, thank you kindly."

The wide mouth stretched slightly as if to start a smile that went nowhere. Pale, unwinking eyes did not change. They assessed everything—saddles, gun-belts, the worn holsters secured by leg ties.

"Nice evening," the rider remarked. "I was playing to it, sort of. Mind if I light down?"

"Suit yourself. You're welcome to a bite of rabbit."

The rider stepped down, all six-four of him. "Just a swig of coffee, if there is any left."

The partners were admiring the mighty horse, sixteen hands high, midnight black save for a forehead star. Dust clung to the sweat of hard travel. Not so long ago he had been run.

Pinkham swished out his cup, scalded it with a splash from the pot, and filled it two thirds full. "Let's all squat. I've been riding all day. My feet are tired."

The stranger did not smile. He found a flat rock and sat on it, not close, giving himself room, keeping the walnut handle of his pistol in the clear. "Lonesome country. Not much going and coming. You're the first ones I've seen today."

Pinkham nodded. "Glad you stopped by. We were getting tired of looking at each other."

The visitor was sipping. "Hot. Just the way I like it. And strong."

"Like yourself," Enright said. "They didn't wean you early. I guess you to be about one-ninety."

"Your business weighing beef on the hoof?"

"I've bought a few."

Willows put down the empty cup. "That cut the

dust. Much obliged. You on a buying trip?"

"We're on a trip," Enright acknowledged. "I've got so I don't talk about buying until I find out how much the seller is willing to take."

Nothing showed in the pale eyes. "Main reason I rode in, gents, was not to beg for coffee. I'm like the gent who knew where he was but didn't know where was was. Know anything about this country?"

Pinkham answered. "Been several years since I was in this far. I worked for a fellow name Fritz Hein when I was younger."

The pale eyes held. "Hein? Seems like I've heard that name somewhere. Is he a stockman?"

"From the old country. He married a rich wife."

Enright grinned. "That's a nice way to get rich. Of course I never saw her. I've never been out this way before."

"Is the Hein outfit on ahead?" the stranger inquired. "That where you're going?"

"I've heard he don't take to strangers," Enright countered. "You lookin' for a job?"

"You mean a gun job?"

"I didn't mean anything. Just talkin'. You already mentioned the weather, so that's been taken care of."

The visitor looked down his long thin nose. "M-m-m, so I did. Well, it has been a long day. I'll mosey along. Thanks again for the coffee. Appreciate it."

"I notice you came off without a bedroll," Enright drawled. "Hope you don't have far to go."

The tall man seemed to study him. "In this country everything is far until you get there."

He went over to the horse, stepped into the saddle, lifted a hand in salute and rode out of the arroyo. The two men stood to watch him go. He did not look back.

"Trustful soul," Enright murmured, "turning his back on us. What was he lookin' for?"

Both men were reflective as they bedded down for the night. Pinkham's badinage wasn't up to par when he opined that Enright hunted around for the softest rock from which to count sheep. He himself lay on his blankets, counting nothing, though there were stars aplenty. Restive, he sat up, careful not to disturb the sleeping Enright, pulled on his boots and walked down to the creek grass, moving slowly through the misty dark. There was a hint of coolness in the air, caressing the skin, drifting toward the Sierra Madres.

He spoke as he neared the horses, calling them by name. As if in response to his voice, there came a faint and distant strain.

He heard the harp again.

Pinkham wandered for a while, then went back to camp.

2

Next morning as they were about to leave, Pink-ham called attention to a band of horsemen who had just broken into view at the creek crossing.

They watched the oncoming riders. "They've spotted us, Joe. Not a bunch of cowhands. Could be a posse."

"Or a bunch of outlaws. They got up before the rooster crowed—if they brought along a rooster."

"They did. That fellow riding at the front is Dean Dalke."

"Ho-ho, so that's Dalke. Big shot in Steamboat Springs. They're ridin' like git-thar and go-to-it. Does Dalke know you?"

"Maybe by name. Might be wise not to mention it, if you can be wise."

"You reckon that important dude would round up a posse to run down his wife?"

"Could be he don't want to go into the Hein place alone. I don't. That's why I made a long ride to tear you away from a passle of cows."

"You're a big lie teller. You like nothin' better than to plot against my peace of mind."

"That's what you've got—a piece of mind."

The eight riders neared, two in the lead. Light reflected momentarily from a badge on the vest of the lead rider at the left.

"I've seen that one, too," Pinkham observed. "Deputy sheriff. He likes to pick fights when he is sure to win. Notice how Dalke rides? That expresses the man. He pushes at everything. Rides like he is shoving the horse along. He really is a big shot, Joe. Has his finger in a lot of pies. Carries a lot of weight."

"Crawlin' crawdads, the deputy has pulled his gun! That's one way for a man to get himself killed. Don't he have any sense at all?"

"Like I said, he is the majority. Play it safe and stand on the off side of your horse. We can talk across the saddles. Let me do the talking."

"You always do. That's what gets me into trouble."

The riders halted, then fanned out in a half-circle in obedience to an order from Dalke. They bristled with weapons. The deputy sat rigidly, the pistol barrel eased across the saddle in front of him. There wasn't much of either man for him to see. Legs, and a pair of faces.

"If they start to cut up, I'm gonna plug him first," Enright whispered. "He looks like a snake in britches."

They waited for the imperious man to speak. He

looked authoritarian. In contrast to the work garb of the others, he was dressed in what Enright called "store clothes"—a long, loose linen coat, mouse-gray pants and polished tooled-leather boots. He didn't greet them. He demanded, "Who are you men? What are you doing here?"

"Tending to our business, mostly," Pinkham replied mildly. "What's your excuse for being here?"

The deputy's thin face puckered as if he were in deep pain. His flesh was too heavily tanned to reveal a flush, but temper was displayed in his outburst.

"Nobody talks that way to Dean Dalke when I'm around. You answer what he asks you, feller, or you got trouble with me."

"There were two questions," Pinkham stated easily. "I answered one. Mr. Dalke didn't answer mine."

"He don't have to answer nothin'!"

"Take it easy, Sid," Dalke rapped out. "Maybe I did rush things. We're wrought up, stranger. We're chasing a horse thief. He can't be too far away. We gave him a hard run before he escaped us."

"It's a big country, Mr. Dalke. Lots of places to hide. I see the man with the badge is all set to shoot the miscreant when he crawls out from behind a rock."

Someone in the crowd laughed, but when the deputy glared around no smiles were visible. Small eyes gleamed at Pinkham.

"Willows was headed this way along that crick when we seen him last. Don't know how you missed seein' him."

"Oh, is his name Willows? My partner sleeps sound. A whole herd could have passed along last night without him knowing. How many horses did Willows steal?"

"One," Dalke answered tersely. "Mine. A black with a star on his forehead. Willows broke out of jail. He was arrested for shooting one of the deputy sheriffs. In the back, if I may say so."

"Calls himself Will of the Willows," the deputy added. "What is your name, feller?" he inquired of Enright. "You there. Yeah, I mean you."

Enright dipped his head toward Pinkham. "I'm with him. George Washington Sudbury the first."

The rider with the funny bone whooped. "Gawd, what a moniker!"

A frown bunched the deputy's eyebrows. He had eyes like a rattlesnake and a mouth like Miss Prim. He was unkempt and looked underfed. Enright stalled his next question by inquiring, "What's your name, buster?"

Before the deputy could think of anything sufficiently scathing, Dalke stated curtly, "Sid Durham, deputy sheriff. We're a stipulated law body. We have the right to ask questions."

"Willows made off with Mr. Dalke's fine hoss,"

the deputy mouthed. "He plays a mouth harp."

"I never heard a horse do that," Enright marveled. "No wonder Mr. Dalke is so hot on the trail."

Dalke abruptly reined his horse around, the bit twisting its lower jaw. "Come on, men! There's nothing to be learned here. Most likely these men are outlaws themselves."

Following his lead, the horsemen rattled away.

Enright looked at Pinkham. "Jail buster, eh! Maybe I shouldn't have sassed them, but I figured you don't want any truck with Dalke just now. Willows plumb neglected to tell us his side of the story. Will of the Willows. That's a dinger."

"It's just as well we didn't blab. I'm not ready to take sides with Dalke on anything. I've heard he has used Durham before when he needed some law weight on his side. Well, Joe, things get curiouser and curiouser."

Enright topped his horse. "Looks like we're all headed to the Hein ranch to jump into the same stew. Dalke's woman hires a young buck to bring you a scribble from Mrs. Hein. The lady says she is dying. Before she kicks off she wants to see Mrs. Dalke. Give her some money, she writes. Wants you to come along. You go to Steamboat Springs to check with Mrs. Dalke. She ain't home. She has run off from her husband, maybe to go see Mrs. Hein. You and Hein hate each other. You say he tried to kill you once, so you'll never get in there alone. So you come to my ranch and talk me into goin' along. Now we get visited by a jail buster and Big Duck Dalke hisself. *And a posse.* I wish I had stayed home."

They rode down out of the arroyo, the pack mare following like a faithful dog, without a lead rope.

3

On a glorious afternoon, they came upon a valley that might have been created from the stuff of dreams. The gracious pines on the westward slopes stood in velvet shadows. To the east their less stately counterparts were interspersed with the gray of aspens. Beyond a green knoll ahead, the tops of a cluster of great cottonwoods attested to the presence of a stream. As the riders climbed, the roof gables of two buildings lifted to peer above the knoll.

Pinkham commented that, after the wild terrain through which they had come, the valley reminded him of his last visit to the Garden of Eden. Whereupon Enright inquired, "How does it feel to be a snake? This valley would feed a thousand head. I don't see even one."

"Fritz Hein pastures on the benchlands at this time of year. His crew spends summers away from the valley."

"Pink, I've been wondering whether Dalke's wife told him about Mrs. Hein's letter. Maybe they had a fuss because he wouldn't allow her to go see Mrs. Hein."

"Could be. "It's not a love marriage, Joe. Dalke bought her from Fritz Hein. Hein bought her from her parents. They were poor Chinese smuggled into this country and left destitute."

Enright looked dumbfounded. "You said she is Dalke's *wife*."

"Maybe marriage was part of the deal. I don't know, but I know that money changed hands. I was working here when Hein bought Lotus Flower from her parents. I thought she was the most beautiful girl I ever saw. I've seen no one since who changed my mind."

"I suppose we'd got rid of buying and selling people. My pappy fought a war about that."

"According to Lotus, poor Chinese don't want girl babies. There are few ways for them to earn a living. Lotus spent most of her childhood in a mission school. Some shyster convinced her parents they could get rich in America. They were brought in like cattle, and wound up dead broke and homeless in a strange country. To them, selling Lotus was a blessing. I don't know what all Hein had in mind when he bought her, but his wife needed help as her ranch work increased. She cooked for the crew and kept house. He strutted around in fine clothes and played big shot. He is the main reason I don't like big shots. I'd like to step on him and squash him like a doodlebug. Only he isn't squash-able. He is as strong as a bull and as tough as whang leather. Faith Hein! Isn't that some name for a woman who had known little but work, work, work?"

"Some folks expect better conditions in heaven. That's faith. I don't know the German name for it."

"I asked her about that. She said her mother worked for an English family. Some official stationed in Germany. They had a child named Faith that the German girl took care of. When she married and had a child of her own—well, that's the answer."

"How much did Hein pay for Lotus?"

"She doesn't know. Seems strange, but she doesn't resent her parents selling her. It was a way for her to help them."

"Some way! Hein got himself a handmaiden like some of the big shots in the Bible."

"She expected something of the kind. Hein never bothered her that way. If he had, I think I would have shot him. There was a feeling between Lotus and me right from the start, as if we reached out to each other. Not lovey-dovey stuff. Affection; a bond. She was only thirteen when she came."

"And you were an old man of—what, about eigh-teen?"

"About that. I wasn't the only one who fell for Lotus. The men liked the girl. Hein wouldn't allow us to talk to her except at mealtimes while she helped serve. The Heins never had any children. Mrs. Hein took the girl to her heart. I think she was starved for someone to love. She certainly didn't love Hein. You should have seen her and Lotus together, heard them! Neither of the Heins speak good English, the woman less than the man. Lotus is unusually bright. She must have soaked in what those mission people taught her. She could rattle away in American better than either of the Heins."

"How long did you know her at the ranch?"

"About two years. Mrs. Hein knew how we felt about each other. She managed things so we could talk together when Hein wasn't around and I was working near the buildings. I was a good worker, so Hein and I got along all right until one day when he caught me talking with Lotus in the barn. He made some remarks about her that made me want to kill him. But it was Hein who nearly killed me. I was so mad that I fought him on his own terms."

They had stopped their horses atop the knoll, where they sat looking at the spread near the cottonwood trees.

Enright heaved a mighty sigh. "I'd give a dollar to own this place."

"Take warning, friend. Such wishes can empty a man's veins."

The low, sprawling house faced the gentle curve of a creek. Grass grew to the stream side; the banks were cleared of boscage. A barn which stood a long hundred yards from the house was equally neat, the adjoining corrals impeccably fenced. Like the house, the structure was low, so wide the roof had little pitch. There were covered cattle runs at each side. The usual ranch litter was missing. Not an item of idle machinery was in view.

"The horse pasture is off to the east," Pinkham said. "The lane leads off from the smaller corral. Not a horse in sight."

"Nor anything else that moves. Let's hear you explain that."

"Reception committee. Dalke dropped off a man to keep track of us."

They rode down-grade, taking their time, the pack mare peacefully trailing, content to go where the other horses went. There was no reason for her to be afraid.

The house nestled lazily in the bright sunlight. At the rear a long ell extended westward from the square main structure. There was no outward indication that men waited beneath its rooftree or watched through its windows; no tendril of rising smoke.

"Nervous fingers are quick on the trigger," Enright said. "I figure that deputy likes to shoot."

"Maybe so, but he has no reason to shoot at us. Not yet, anyway."

"Blast it, George Washington, pull down your hat like I told you to. Be yourself and hump down like a starving range bum, if you can fold your belly. They're probably lookin' at us through a pair of field glasses."

"George Washington. How come you thought to call me that?"

"You're not tall enough for Abe. Still no sign of life at the house. I'll bet you they're itching to know who we are and what we want. How do you aim to handle this?"

"Play the cards as they fall. Hitch up your courage and pray."

Nothing happened to change the outward scene until their horses ambled past the barn. Both building faced the creek.

"The back door is open," Enright commented. "No screen."

As he spoke, a man stepped into the open.

"Fritz Hein," Pinkham informed Enright. "He is giving us the evil eye."

"Knickers!" Enright marveled. "I can see the shine on his boots from here. Crawlin' crawdads, he is wearing a watch chain. Lawdy-daw!"

If Hein were armed, the weapon did not show. His coal-black hair was neatly combed, parted precisely in the middle. The upturned ends of his black mustache were waxed to militant points. Slightly protuberant blue eyes were glaring at Pinkham.

"His temper is colored red," Pinkham said, low.

"Watch him heat up when he figures out who I am. Oh-oh—he knows!"

"Halt vere you are!" the rancher called out loudly. "Pingham, I tolt you to shtay off my landt."

The voice was harsh, guttural, but Hein was not hard to understand. Neither was his manner. He was the general.

They stopped their horses thirty feet away from him. Pinkham spoke respectfully.

"Mr. Hein, that was a long time ago. Circumstances are different now. We are here on business."

"I haff no pizness mit you. Get oudt!"

"I am a U. S. marshal. This is my deputy, Joe Enright. I received a letter from Mrs. Hein stating that she wants to see me. That is why we are here."

Hein's bulky shoulders braced as if snapped by a strong spring. He stood speechless and incredulous for a moment, the blue eyes swelling in their sockets. As Pinkham had predicted, color climbed into his face. He stuttered a bit, then burst into speech.

"Vot iss ziss you say, *Frau* Hein does not ledders write. No ledders haff go avay from ziss ranch. I know effrysing about that."

Pinkham stepped down from the saddle. Enright also dismounted. Back of the rancher, the blocky, assertive figure of Dean Dalke came through the doorway. "Marshals!" he exclaimed. "Do I understand that you are Marshal Sudbury Pinkham?"

"Correct. And this is Joe Enright. He owns a small

ranch West of Steamboat Springs. A former governor's deputy. Perhaps you have heard of him?"

Dalke frowned. "You men deceived me when I accosted you. I want to know why. Respectable peace officers are not ashamed of their identity."

"You accosted us, as you just said," Pinkham replied mildly. "Perhaps that is why."

Dalke did not look abashed. He winced, however, when Fritz Hein spoke harshly. "I deal with ziss meinself. Ziss is my property. Pingham, vot you say aboudt ledders? You got no ledders from *Frau* Hein."

Pinkham dipped two fingers into a vest pocket and brought forth a folded paper. He opened it, holding it so Hein could see, stepping back as the rancher reached for it.

"Don't touch! Read it, if you can read."

"Let me see that thing!" Dalke demanded abruptly, shouldering past Hein, drawing a baleful glance. Pinkham allowed him to take the paper.

"Be very, very careful with it, Mr. Dalke. Read it to him, but don't let him lay hands on it."

Dalke gave him a hard stare, then looked at the paper.

LIEBSCHEN: I DIE. COME QUICK.
I HAVE MONEY FOR YOU.
FIND THE PINKHAM BOY. BRING HIM.
FAITH.

He read the message aloud, translating the scribbled, misspelled words. Hein exploded.

"Money! Faith has no moneys! That iss a lie Giff me—"

Enright's pistol slid smoothly from its holster. "Uh-uh!" he warned. "Mind what Pinky says. Don't touch."

Dalke had stepped away from the angry rancher. "Pinkham, where did you get this paper?"

"It was sent to me by your wife. Give it back, please. Let's not have trouble."

Dalke surrendered the message reluctantly. "You're hardly a boy. Did Faith know you when you were a boy?"

"I worked for Hein when I was eighteen. Didn't your wife mention hearing from Mrs. Hein?"

"I doubt that is any of your business."

"Maybe not. Mrs. Hein sent the message to her, and she hired a man to bring it to me. When I went to see her about it, I found out that she had left home. Did she tell you she was coming to see Mrs. Hein? Is that why you're here? Waiting for your wife *with a posse*? She must have become a dangerous woman since I saw her last."

"When was that?" Dalke demanded sharply, his cheeks flushing.

"Never mind. Is there some connection between the man Willows and your wife?"

"I do not shtand here und listen to ziss stuff!"

Hein shouted. "Dalke, you tagk your men oudt of here. Villows vill nodt come here. If he does I vill shoodt him."

"Then you know Willows?" Pinkham shot at him. *"Who is he?"*

"A crook who shoudt be in chail, like he was till he got oudt. I vant nodding to do mit Villows."

Pinkham turned to Dalke. "Do you know who he is?"

"Only what my wife told me. I understand that he brought word to her that Mrs. Hein was sick. I didn't know anything about that paper. We never discussed it. I caught Willows hanging around my place. When I accosted him, he attacked me. Later, when I sent men to arrest him, he shot a deputy. He is a dangerous man, Marshal. I told you he broke jail and that he stole one of my horses. You should be devoting your time to him, not to badgering honest people."

Pinkham looked at Hein. "I came here to talk with your wife. Do you consider that being badgered?"

Hein turned his back and marched into the house. It was an angry back, stiff and unyielding.

"Don't push him," Dalke warned. "You will get nowhere. Is this an official visit? Do you have a warrant of some kind?"

"I don't," but I intend to see Mrs. Hein."

"She isn't here. She left while Hein was away in town. He says he doesn't know where she went.

I believe him. He is boiling about it."

"Is it true that she is ill, perhaps dying?"

"I wouldn't know. He doesn't admit it."

"I don't want to butt into your family business, Mr. Dalke. Did your wife tell you she was coming to see Mrs. Hein?"

He flushed again. "We quarreled about it," he said bitterly. "I refused to let her come out here. I'd think she would have no love for this place, but she seems to idolize Mrs. Hein. She ran away. It isn't the first time. We don't get along too well, I must admit. Not that it is any of your business. But you can snoop around and find out, so I might as well tell you. Is there something else you want to know?"

Pinkham ignored the sarcasm. "Ran away with what? What did she use for transportation?"

"She took our horse and buggy."

"Do you think she came and took Mrs. Hein away?"

"I know she didn't. Mrs. Hein has been gone for some time. I understand that she was mulish because Hein was bringing in another woman to do her work. She didn't take a rig. She left on her favorite horse. An old one, gentle to ride."

"Where would a sick woman go?"

"Hein thinks she is with the crew. He isn't worried."

"He wasn't worried. He is now. The woman's message upset him. What is the trouble between him and Willows?"

"I don't know. Look, Marshal, I've tried to be decent about this. I don't have to answer your questions. There is nothing more for you here. Please go away. The harm is already done. Willows will never come here now. We might as well all leave."

"Sorry to have sprung your trap. Joe and I didn't know who it was sent for us, Willows or your wife. Seems a man wouldn't need the help of a posse to take his wife back home."

"I've had enough of your impertinence." Dalke snapped. "Get out of here, both of you. And stay away from my wife."

He about-faced abruptly and went into the house.

Pinkham and Enright looked at each other, grinned and climbed into their saddles. "Come on, Nancy," Enright said to the pack mare. "Let's do as the man says."

As they rode toward the knoll, he prodded Pinkham with a question. "Ever have the feeling you're being watched from behind by someone who would like to shoot you? That mean-eyed deputy is in the kitchen. I saw him peekin' out a window, along with a redheaded woman. Whoever she is, she ain't Faith Hein. This one ain't lean and worked to the bone like you described Mrs. Hein. She is well fed and in full bloom. I suppose there is no sense trying to find Willows?"

"He probably knows every move we've made. Only way we'd find him would be if he wants to be found, and I don't believe he does. I'm hungry. Let's find a place to camp. There used to be a good spring in a glade up in the east timber. Cattle trample it when they're around. Now it should be clear and cool."

"Well, we found out Mrs. Dalke hasn't showed up yet. Maybe she will be smart enough to stay away. What do you think?"

"She might not come if she finds out about Dalke. Otherwise, there is no reason for her to be afraid to come here. Anxiety about Mrs. Hein will determine what she does. I think she will come. I'm surprised she hasn't done so already."

"Would she know how to get here?"

"I doubt it. That probably explains why she hasn't appeared. Dalke's men are staying under cover despite what he said about leaving. I suppose the rest of them are in the barn."

The southern portion of the valley lay behind them now; the buildings were out of sight beyond the rise. Walking hooves were muffled by tufted grass, and the summer breeze was no more than the rustle of a wing. Above and beyond them at the left, a grove of aspens whitened the mountain greenery.

"The spring is up that way," Pinkham said, pointing. "Tonight I'm going to take my bedroll and stake out up this side of that rise. If Lotus is in a buggy, she wouldn't come in from the foothills. She will come in just like we did. I don't want her to go to the house alone."

"I'll go along and sleep while you use your big owl eyes to see in the dark. If she doesn't know the country, it isn't likely she will do any traveling after dark."

"She knows the valley. Besides, there will be light until ten or eleven o'clock. The moon is in the first quarter."

"Then I'll take the first watch, and you'll take the owl watch, and we'll both get to Scotland together," Enright sang in a passable baritone.

Shortly after the two men were out of sight in the timber, a black horse came out of the trees farther on. He crossed the grassland, moving westward with a smooth, swinging stride. When he came to the far slope, Willows guided him upward, weaving through trees and undergrowth until he nosed out a small depression where a buggy stood almost buried amid surrounding brush. A dun horse tied nearby pricked its ears and whinnied softly. The animals recognized each other. Both belonged to Dean Dalke.

Dismounting, Willows led the black into undergrowth where he could not be seen from the depression. Tying him, the man in black sought a spot where he could stretch out in comfort and settled down to wait.

4

Pinkham was being nostalgic. "I've seen this valley covered with cattle. It was a fair sight, with plenty of grass, the sky as blue as a mountain lake, water in the creek, my life in the springtime."

"The sky was blue today and the grass up to our stirrups," Enright commented without poesy in his soul. "Now that you're an old man, how about telling me what happened between you and Fritzy Hein back there in the springtime? What gave you such high opinions of each other?"

They were stretched out on their bedrolls on the north slope of the knoll, a short way below the crest. Night had come. A pale disk floated in the cloudless sky.

"I hired out to him when I was a sprout," Pinkham said somewhat dreamily. "I didn't know much, but I was full of beans. Thought I could whip anything my size that walked on two legs and ride anything that ran on four. Had some fights; never got licked. That's bad for a youngster. Liable to make him cocky. I thought I was pretty good with a hand gun. Never drew on a man in those days. Never had to. That was before you hired me to help out on a case and taught me bad habits."

"I also taught you never to pull a gun unless your mind was made up to use it if you had to."

"Yeah. You're smart in some ways. Joe, you wouldn't believe what Hein can do with a bull whip. He can snake a lash within an inch of your nose and never touch you."

"I wouldn't trust him to do that. I like my nose. It keeps my eyes apart."

"When Hein has trouble with a man, he doesn't settle with fists or guns. Oh, he might use a gun to make you get rid of yours, then toss you a whip. I think he would fight a man with a whip even though he knew he might get licked. Enjoys it. Likes to see blood run. I've seen him fight, and I've seen him hurt, but I've never seen him beat. I've also seen him fight for sport, but with Hein fun can turn bloody."

"I can understand that. His temper flares like a prairie fire."

"I think he is twisted. He is a mean devil when he gets mad. He sure blew off when he caught Lotus and me in the barn. We were being perfectly respectable. By his lights, women were created to serve men. He never did any of the hard work. Dressed up. Gave orders. Mrs. Hein worked like a dog on a treadmill. I doubt he ever noticed."

"Quite a spot for a thirteen-year-old girl."

"Would have been worse except for Mrs. Hein. She is a strange, silent woman. I think she buried herself in work in order to take her mind off Hein. She never said anything against him where I could hear it. Probably she sounded off to Lotus, although she is not the talking kind. She liked me. Seemed to understand how Lotus and I felt about each other. I believe it pleased her. Lotus was just a kid, but in some ways she seemed more like a woman."

"Some children grow up faster than others. Seems like that sort of experience would make a kid hard."

"It didn't affect Lotus that way. Made her wiser, undoubtedly, but certainly not hard. She is a serene person. I've mentioned that she spent a good part of her early childhood at a mission school. She is intelligent. Apparently she had good teachers. She talks as well as you or I."

"Which ain't saying too much. What did Hein think about you and the girl?"

"There wasn't anything between us except feeling. Lotus helped in the kitchen and with the housework. Hein wouldn't let her visit with us. Didn't want the men to do more than speak to her. I was a good worker, so for quite a while we got along fine. Then one day he caught me talking with Lotus in the barn. What he said about Lotus made me want to fight him. I'd have fought him with tooth-picks. There is a sort of cellar room off that ell on the west side of the house. A hall connects with the bunkhouse and leads on to the room. We went into that room to have it out. I was as prancy as a stallion looking over a fence at a bunch of fillies. Joe, I didn't know anything about whip fighting. The big devil got me in there, tossed me a whip and peeled off his shirt. In twenty minutes he would have had me in ribbons."

"Long on muscles, short on sense. Matched against a pro."

"That room has no windows. He lit a lamp on a high shelf near the door. Man, we had a hell of a time. He thrust the lash at me like a striking rat-ler. In five minutes I realized I was nothing but a hot-headed young fool. Instead of trying to work on him, I knocked the lamp off the shelf. It busted and set fire to the oil. All at once Hein had something to think about besides skinning me alive. He shot me as I went out of there like a singed rabbit. Joe, I don't know to this day how I managed to lock the door. It didn't hold him long. He was like a mean old range bull. He was out and shooting when I rode up the other side of this knob. I had to leave my war bag and all my extra duds. Lost almost a months' pay. If my horse hadn't been already sad-dled, Hein would have killed me. He almost did, anyway."

"Too bad you didn't take the girl with you."

"She wouldn't have left Mrs. Hein. I came back twice after that. The first time I sneaked in at night and surprised Hein. I managed to get away in good shape because I never gave him a chance to hurt me. Next time out I brought field glasses, the ones we have now. I waited until everyone but the women was away. Tried to get them to leave with me. Mrs. Hein wouldn't, and Lotus refused to desert her. Riding away and leaving them was the hardest thing I had ever done. I bawled like a kid. Took time before I realized I had scared the women by coming out to see them. They were afraid Hein would find out they had talked to me."

"You said he shot you. Whereabouts?"

"Joe, I hardly felt it until I was halfway out of the valley. First thing I realized was that my leg felt wet. I stopped and tied myself up with my shirt and undershirt. Good thing. I would have bled to death. Took me three days to make it to Hahn's Peak, and three months before I could walk down a street without falling on my face. I wound up homeless, broke and without a job. That's how I happened to start reading law with Judge Toomey. I did flunky work to pay for my keep."

"Didn't know you could read."

"I wasn't good at it. I learned a lot while I was with the judge, but not enough to stay away from gents like you."

"Nor from Fritz Hein. How come Lotus knew where to find you?"

"I saw her once after she married Dalke. I was in Steamboat Springs. Saw them riding together in a buggy. I never got struck by lightning, but by dogies, I know how it feels. She saw me, too. For a minute her face lighted up like a sunrise. I know she started to call out to me. But she didn't. Her eyes shut, and she looked like she was going to cry. I asked around and found out Dalke had married a Chinese. You know how nice white folks look down their noses at such things. But Dalke is a big shot. They wouldn't say anything to his face."

"Kind of like the ending of a nice dream. Only you're not over it. She hollers help, and you jump on your bronc and ride in all directions."

"Yeah. Well, it's time to shut up. If you're bound to take the first watch, I'm gonna get some sleep."

"Up to now I've hardly said a word. Think I'll go up on top where I can see the buildings."

"You couldn't see anybody that far away."

"It will get me where I won't have to listen to you."

"Unless something happens to scare you, don't wake me until daylight."

"I'll wake you when the moon goes down so you can use your owl eyes."

Enright was sound asleep in his own bedroll when Pinkham rudely shook him awake. He came up fighting, thinking he was being attacked.

"Snap out of it, Joe! Hell has broke loose down by the buildings. Shooting all over the place. Willows has made his move."

They ran together toward the top of the rise, and had no more than gotten there when a rush of hooves below caused them to scuttle away to the side like rabbits flushed by a pack of hounds.

"What's going on?" Enright panted. "That bunch nearly ran us down. They must be chasing Willows."

"Dang it, what happened to my glasses?"

"You had them. I didn't."

"Dang it, I'm not going to lose my good glasses."

"You probably laid them down by the blankets when you went to work on me. You were banging my head on the ground like you'd gone crazy."

"I was not. Let's go look. I don't want to lose those glasses."

"Do it yourself. I'm not gonna crawl for you. That bunch is still going lickety-clatter. Pink, the house is dark. Seems like I see a light in the barn."

"Watch it so it won't go away," Pinkham said sarcastically. He was on the way down-slope. He apparently had some difficulty locating the place where they had spread their bedrolls, for he was gone for some time and had to call out in order to locate Enright when he returned to the crest of the knoll. He had found the glasses.

"Don't hear anything from off north now. They

either stopped or rode out of hearing."

"The light came around back of the barn, then went out."

"Now you're seeing lights with legs. Something funny going on down there. The whole place is dark now."

"I'll swear I heard Willows' mouth harp. Just a little dab before the light went out. Do you suppose—"

"That he chased Dalke's outfit out of the barn? No, I don't. You sure you heard him?"

"No, I'm not. It was prob'ly a band of angels rehearsin' for Christmas. You want to go down there and find out?"

"It wasn't Lotus who set off the fireworks. They wouldn't shoot at her. Whatever happened, that bunch wasn't chasing a buggy."

"Ho-up! Listen!"

They stood in silence, invisible to each other in the dark.

"Another horse," Enright said. "This one ain't in a hurry. Maybe we ought to get over there and stop him."

"I don't care how many of them leave. It's what goes in that interests me."

"You ain't as curious as I am. What kind of shooting was it? Six-guns? Rifles?"

"Cannons. What difference does it make? It's not long until daylight. I'm going down to the barn while I can still make it in the dark. I'm sure Dalke's outfit has cleared out."

"Some of them, anyway."

"I think we ought to be ready to move. Something has broke loose. I don't know what. Let's not get caught on foot. Go back to the camp and pack our gear. It will be light by the time you get back here. Better pick up our bedrolls and tie them on. Don't ride down to the buildings unless I give you a sign."

"How you gonna do that? Tie your shirt tail to a fishing pole?"

"At daylight I'll come out back of the barn."

"Suppose Hein is sittin' on your belly, making mincemeat of your face?"

"I'll take care of myself. You do the same. Watch out for that horse gang. Make sure they're not in sight when you come out of the woods."

"Suppose they are? What do I do then—climb a tree and build a nest?"

"You ride out and make faces at them to scare them away. Just be natural. That will do the trick. Get going! And *be careful*."

5

If appearances could be trusted, the night was replete with peace in the valley of Fritz Hein. Southward, below the knoll north of which Pinkham and Enright had spread out their bedrolls, light from the moon faintly bathed the buildings with soft radiance. The low, wide barn huddled in shadows beneath the moonlit roof. The near windows of the unlighted house, untouched by moonlight, lost their identity in the dark façades of the walls. Pale light traced the outlines of the empty corrals. Night creatures prowled unseen.

"Hein hates dogs," Pinkham had told his partner. "No stray ever came to that place and stayed alive."

Near the witching hours, the lowering moon seemed to float above the skyline, hesitant to dip below the high ridges of the earth. Shadows from the buildings reached out long fingers. When the silvery mirror in the sky sank from view, a slim figure came out of hiding below the creek bank and crouched upon the grassland. At about the same time three men came out of the barn. They led a string of saddle horses to a watering trough in the smaller corral. One man climbed upon the platform of a well and worked the handle of a pump while the animals drank. The men were not noisy about the chore. They had waited for the full descent of darkness. The buildings were now hidden by the cloak of night.

Pinkham's surmise had been correct. Dalke's men were staying under cover in the barn.

The watcher in the grass waited until men and horses were inside the barn again, then drifted toward the house. There followed an interval of listening as the darkness deepened and stars brightened in the dusky sky. Having lost its celestial lantern, the earth turned on toward the morn.

On cat feet the phantom figure flitted around the house to an open window at the west and crouched below the sill. Beyond the window the room lay in darkness. There were no sounds of slumber. A leg lifted across the sill with no more than a sneaky rustle, and the window was as it had been before. The night creature was inside the room.

How could a room be so quiet in the presence of the living? The sleep of innocence is not the stillness of the dead. There are small sounds—the indrawn breath, the pulsing heart, the shiftings in slumber. Fritz Hein's household breathed deceit.

Feet whispered across the floor. Legs brushed the side of a bed. Hands reached forth to explore.

Quick little touches moved upward to locate the sleeper's face and clamp a hand firmly over the women's mouth. Instantly the intruder was kneeling beside the bed, and face was pressed to face.

"Faith, Faith, don't be scared. Don't make a sound. I'm here. I'm here."

The insistent whisper into the shell of an ear could not have been heard outside the room. For the woman in the bed, the clamping hand might have awakened terror. But there was no convulsive awakening, no strangling breath. Strong hands came up to grasp a wrist. A twisting pull, a thrusting shoulder was flung across the bed, threshing wildly to break free.

Swiftly stillness changed to bedlam, the gaspings of violent struggle, a woman's yells. Elsewhere the house awoke to other sounds—the voices of men, the stir of movement, feet thumping across the floor. A match flared; a lamp wick steadied into a glow.

Frizt Hein strode into the bedroom, one hand grasping the slender stem below the bowl of a kerosene lamp. Dean Dalke was close upon his bare heels. Both men were clad in light underwear. Their hair was tousled, their eyes puffy from sleep.

"Help me!" came a panting appeal from the heaving tangle on the bed. "I can't hold her much longer."

Hein started to put down the lamp on a dresser

top, but Dalke thrust past him. "Hold the light. I'll tend to her."

Striding to the bed, he tore the combatants apart and roughly flung one to the floor. A voice cried out in pain when a flailing arm struck a corner of the dresser. The intruder squirmed about and came up as lithely as a cat. Great eyes flared at Dalke; then the woman, clad like a man, darted toward the open window. Dalke hauled her back from behind. She was wiry, she was frightened, she was desperate. With considerable difficulty he forced her against a wall and managed to hold her there as resistance drained away.

"I'm torn to pieces," moaned the woman on the bed. "She is the devil's own."

The great eyes were ignoring Dalke and Hein. They stared at the other woman. In the lamplight they reflected a cat-like sheen.

"Where is Mama Faith?"

Dalke's hands clamped her shoulders, shaking her. "I told you not to come here. You disobeyed me again. What must I do to make you mind? Lock on a ball and chain?"

She looked at him, her eyes appealing. "Do not make me go back. I am no good for you."

Hein placed the lamp on a chest of drawers. "I vill talk mit liddle Lotus. I fix things for you, Dalke. You vill see."

Her look scorned him. "You sold me like a cow.

I went with him because you said I must. I was frightened on account of Mama Hein."

"Now, now, liddle Lotus, you coom mit me. Ve haff a liddle talk about how you haff been a bad girl."

"Never mind about that," Dalke objected when Hein laid hold of his arm to pull him away from the girl. "I'll do my own talking."

"I haff her pefore you. I know vot to do."

He bulled Dalke aside, latching a great paw on the girl's wrist. The woman sitting in the bed watched avidly, her back propped against the headboard, a rumpled sheet clutched over ample breasts. Tangled red hair peered from beneath a lace nightcap, framing a round face centered by a rosy pug nose, presided over by wide set large green eyes. Bee-stung lips glistened as she moistened them with a pink tongue.

The girl braced against the wall, resisting Hein's pull, but he dragged her away. The flushed Dalke balled his fists. He glanced uncertainly at the woman when she asked eagerly, "What you gonna do to her, Fritz?"

"Neffer you mind. Gedt oudt of bed and light my vay. Pick up the lamp. Dalke, you vait in the kitchen. I talk mit liddle Lotus. Venn ve come back, she vill haff changed her mind."

The red head had climbed out of bed. A soft, plump hand took up the lamp.

"Where are you taking her?" Dalke demanded, plainly of a mind to interfere, yet hesitating to do so.

"I got a place. She has been there pefore."

"This is your house. I know Lotus has no right to come here as she did like a thief in the night. I forbade her to come, but she disobeyed. But she is still my wife. I don't want—"

"*Shod up!*" Hein yelled at him, pulling Lotus along a passageway. "You haff been too easy mit her. I know vot to do."

Dalke's eyes glinted. For a moment it seemed he might physically intervene, but he did not follow as the three went off along the passageway, the redhead at the rear, carrying the lamp. Still stubborn, he turned and went slowly toward the kitchen. From there he could not see Hein push the no longer protesting girl down four steps to a landing outside a padlocked door.

Shoving Lotus into a corner, Hein held her there while he reached overhead to remove a key ring from a nail driven into the wall above the door. Imprisoning her with his body, he used the key to unlock the padlock. Leaving the key in the lock, he replaced the key ring on the nail. Opening the door, he shoved Lotus into the dark room.

"Giff me the light," he said to the redhead. "You go bagk to your room unt shtay there."

"Aw, Fritz, let me watch."

She fled when he swore at her. Entering, he closed the door. The low-ceilinged room was large, windowless, thick with heat and closed-in mustiness. A blanket-covered cot occupied one corner, beside it a simple chest of drawers.

Hein placed the lamp on a high shelf beside the door. The moving light revealed two long-lashed bull whips criss-crossed on wall nails below the shelf.

"Tagk off your clothes."

Lotus Flower stood facing him, her back against the far wall. His order stiffened her. Dark eyes examined him as if unwilling to believe what she had heard. "You can whip me as I am. Go ahead if you must."

"Tagk off your clothes."

His voice had taken on a peculiar crooning sound. "I will not!"

"I tear dem off. You vill haff to go aroundt naked."

"If you harm me, I will kill myself."

"*Nein, nein,* liddle Lotus. I not ledt you do that. You haff a bad girl been. You mus' be punished."

The dark eyes feared him, defiance gone. "What do you intend to do?"

"Tagk off your clothes. I tell you no more."

She splayed against the wall as he started forward, her arms outstretched, palms pressing the rough surface. A sob caught in her throat, choking back a scream.

"All right! All right; Stand back. Don't come near me. Don't touch me."

Her frightened gaze fixed on him, she started fumblingly to disrobe. The levis came off first, slipped over shoeless feet. Finally, unclothed, she stood as faraway from Hein as the unyielding wall would permit.

She tried to shrink into the wall as he ambled toward her. But he did not touch her. Instead, he sat on the cot, his knees squeezed tightly together.

"Come to me, Lotus," he commanded thickly. "Bad girls must be spanked."

Desperate eyes sought the door in a frantic search for escape. Yet she was far enough from panic to realize there was no escape. Whatever was to come she must endure. She went and lay across his knees.

Swiftly he was flailing at her, striking as if to punish himself as much as her.

After a first cry she did not utter another sound. He whacked her unmercifully, his flat palm spatting against her bare skin until it was puffed and reddened.

Ceasing, he stood, shunting her body to the floor as he arose. He walked to the shelf without looking at her again, took down the lamp and went away. The trembling girl heard the padlock click.

Moaning, she crawled over to the cot. Kneeling beside it, she hid her face in folded arms.

"Oh, God, help me, help me."

6

Dean Dalke sat astride a kitchen chair. The fingers of a hairy-backed right hand idly turned an empty coffee cup around and around, as if playing a game of their own. Dalke stared at nothing.

His head turned sidewise at the sound of footsteps in the passageway beyond the inner door. Fritz Hein entered. His features were bloated. The disturbing glassy stare fixed on Dalke.

"I pay you bagk," he declared thickly. "Eff'ry cent you giff me."

As if in a daze, he pulled out a chair and plumped upon the seat, a sudden weight that made the legs creak.

"Should neffer have soldt her. Should have kept her vere she belonks. She belonks to me."

"What the devil are you talking about?" Dalke flung at him, knowing very well what he meant and angry because it had been put into words. "If you molested my wife, I'll kill you like a dog."

"Hah! I didn't vip her. I meant to vip her, but I neffer."

"I've been sitting here hating myself because I let you take her away. From now on it's hands off. Understand that, my friend, or you're in trouble."

Hein shook his head from side to side as if to dislodge a weight from his brain. "Ve trade back like it vass. I go gedt your money."

"We'll do no such thing! Lotus belongs to me. Where is she?"

Their eyes did battle, the protuberant orbs feverish, Dalke unyielding. "I didn't come out here to make a trade. You locked her up, didn't you? Hand over the key."

Again a violent negative head shake. *"Nein! Nein!"*

"Be reasonable, man! I don't want to fight you over a woman. I helped you out with Pinkham. I lied for you. I don't like to lie."

"Gedt oud of mine house. You are no longer velcome here."

"That is all right with me, but when I leave Lotus goes along. Give me the key."

"I giff you nodding."

"Then I'll bring in my men from the barn and take it. Come on, man! Stop this madness. You have no more chance with me than a chunk of ice in hell."

Dalke started to get up. In a burst of rage Hein thrust the table against him, upsetting him and his chair. A bracket lamp traced the shadow of Hein's plunging dive. The heavy features had congested. His hand hooked out for Dalke's throat.

"Giff me orders, vill you?" he mouthed. "Call in your schwein to beadt me op? Tagk avay Lotus Flower. She iss mine—she iss mine."

Amid the wreckage of his chair, the surprised Dalke thrust up a fending arm. "*Durham!*" he roared. "Durham! Come here!"

In the next breath he was fighting for his life.

Dean Dalke was strong. He was not a coward. But he was not seasoned in roughhouse brawling. There was nothing ordered about Hein's attack. He swarmed. Hooked fingers raked Dalke's face. They clawed at his throat. Hair as bristly as fine wire stabbed from the cruelly butting head. Hard knee bones rammed the tender groin.

Clutching the compact body which had smashed him to the floor, Dalke tried to unbalance it, twist it aside, roll Hein over on his back. Clamping his chin tight against his chest, he managed to avoid the vising hands that sought to throttle him. And as he fought, a searing thought burned through his brain. Fritz Hein meant to kill him.

Unable to roll Hein aside, he released the body hold to hammer his ribs below the armpits—powerful blows that hurt. Hein's breath was ejected in moaning grunts with every hit, but the brutal attack grew fiercer still. Giving up his hammering, Dalke grasped the thick wrists, but could not tear them away. Pain shot up from his larynx. Breath was trapped in his lungs. Despairing, he rose on his heels, arching his body in an effort to throw Hein over his head. Though not entirely successful, the move shifted the crushing weight enough to provide added leverage. Summoning his failing strength, he flung Hein aside and reared up on tottery legs. Blood dribbled from his mouth. His breathing sounded like the wheezing bellows of a forge.

Hein came up almost as quickly and seemed in better shape. His legs were steady, his face ugly from the emotions that roiled inside. He had never stopped talking, disconnected mouthings about women—his wife—the girl.

On his feet Dalke was a better fighter. There had been no further opportunity to yell for assistance, nor could he now. He was in no shape to yell. The deputy and the other members of the posse were too far away to hear the ruckus. One man would be on watch. The others would be sleeping. There was no help for Dalke. He fought for his life.

The brain accustomed to giving orders and outdealing lesser men strove to bring order to the fight. He bloodied Hein's face, hammered his heart, tried to knock in his ribs, hurting him, staggering him, driving him back again and again. But Hein was a raging beast. Amazingly, his strength seemed to build up as that of Dalke waned, and the struggling defender began to realize he could not win. The realization drained his confidence. His struggle grew desperate, and thereby he hastened his defeat.

Hein soon had him cornered in a last despairing stand. His fists were no longer bruising mauls. He tried to bull out of the trap, only to be flung back against the wall, a human rat, tattered and bloody, his arms leaden, his body sagging, his legs ready to give way. But still he tried.

Remorseless hands brushed away helplessly fending arms, reaching for the squeezing kill.

From outside the open kitchen door came the soft music of a harp. *"Rock of Ages, cleft for me. . . ."*

Feet fluttered along the passageway adjacent to the inside kitchen door, the corridor to the crew's quarters and Hein's prison room of punishment. A girl's face showed for an instant above the flashing outlines of her body, now fully clothed. Her voice wafted in to them.

"I will find out what you did to Mama Faith. Be sure of that."

The clutching hands released their victim. Dalke had sufficient presence of mind to edge out of the corner and move staggeringly toward the outside door. Hein did not attempt to stop him. The rancher stood rooted in his tracks, goggling eyes fixed on the opening where Lotus Flower had showed herself, then disappeared from view. An automaton, his head swiveled on a stiff body to look at the black hole of the night. The deranged features struggled to readjust. Mouth agape, Hein stood amid the wreckage of his kitchen, a bedraggled figure staring into the concealing dark.

The harp had grown silent. His ragged breathing was the only sound.

Shaking himself like a scuffy animal aroused from a long sleep, he stepped over to lift the lamp from its bracket and blow out the flame. Then he stood back against the wall, listening, hearing nothing to intimate their would be a forthcoming attack. Down near the barn, Dean Dalke's voice shouted away the silence.

Hein carefully replaced the lamp. He moved cautiously into the pasageway, distrustful of the silence; on past the kitchen and bunkrooms. A light still burned in the cellar room. The door stood open. Someone had found the key ring or pried off the lock.

He left the passageway to cross a dark room toward a streak of light under a closed door. The knob turned, but the door met resistance inside. Lunging, he shouldered it open, pushing aside the bed which had been moved against it. An open window yawned. The redheaded woman was gone.

Standing at one side, careful not to show himself in the window opening, Hein reached out to close the window. He lowered the blind. Then he picked up the lamp from the dresser top and stood for a full minute inside the door, listening, for movement within the house. Hearing nothing to alarm him, he crossed a center room to pause before another locked door. Using two keys, he unlocked it and went inside. The door was two inches thick, made of solid unpaneled oak.

The windowless room was an arsenal. Wooden racks on the wall facing the door held an assortment of weapons, a single and three double- barreled shotguns, sawed-off weapons wickedly suggestive of close-range death. Four long guns rested in the brackets of a rifle rack, one a handsome, brass-decorated Sharps.

Several cartridge belts hung on the studded pegs of a wooden backboard, pistols in the holsters, with them a smaller weapon in a flat strapped arrangement designed to be worn around the shoulders, concealed beneath a coat. Two derringers and two hunting knives in scabbards lay on a cabinet top. Near them was a sheathless bowie. Hein shoved the great knife aside to make room for the lamp.

The walls bordering the door were draped with long-lashed whips, some slender-handled, others weighted for use as clubs. The ends of one lengthy lash were tipped with thin strips of metal.

Hein selected a Colt .45 in a plain black holster and buckled the belt around his waist. The leather was soft and pliable. All the weapons appeared to have had good care. The bowie knife was honed to a razor edge.

He opened the top drawer of the cabinet, revealing a store of ammunition. From it he filled the cartridge loops of the belt and loaded the pistol. He strapped on the shoulder holster and filled the smaller weapon with shells. From the rifle rack he lifted out a Winchester, worked the action several times, then filled the magazine. Jacking a cartridge into the barrel, he set the safety and was ready to leave.

Hein blew out the light, picked up the bowie knife and went through the door. The clicking of the locks was the only sound, but he waited in the dark for an interval calculated to upset a nervous enemy come to avenge the beating of Dean Dalke.

He knew his way across the room and along the passageway. His big feet were surprisingly quiet. He did not follow the passageway to the kitchen, did not go toward the glow of the open cellar room door. He entered the bedroom where, hours ago, it seemed, the redheaded woman had captured Lotus Flower in her attempt to find his wife.

Again, after cautiously listening, he moved across to the window, opened it slowly and silently eased his muscular body to the ground outside.

Down at the barn, there was a good deal of commotion, voices, sounds of movement, a dim show of light. Dean Dalke's small army was on the move.

Rage flared in him again. Hidden by the dark, the feral creature stalked toward the barn.

7

A voice called hoarsely through the darkness, "Durham—Sid Durham—"

"Wha— Who— Hey, Mr. Dalke, is that you?"

"Light a lantern."

"But you said not to show a light."

"I know what I said. Rouse the men. We're clearing out. Fritz Hein has blown his lid. Gone raving mad."

A match flared and a wick settled into steady glow.

"Cri-min—ee!" gasped the lantern holder. "You look like you been run through a sawmill."

Dalke glared back at the reptilian eyes. He was well aware that the deputy didn't care whether he lived or died, save that no one else would hand out the expected gratuity when the venture was over. Not at all clever at concealing his feelings, Durham was savoring the discomfiture of his master.

I'm beat half to death, Dalke thought bitterly. And he likes it.

Since Durham hadn't done so, Dalke yelled at the men sleeping in various positions in the feedway of the barn. When they awakened to his summons, expecting to engage in acts of violence, he told them to tighten the girths of the already saddled horses and lead them out to the rear of the building. Nobody inquired about the reason for departure, supposing it to be a part of what they had come to do. Durham knew differently. The small eyes kept picking at Dalke. The lick of a coated tongue tasted the boss man's defeat. Durham didn't like Dalke. He didn't like Hein. In fact, he didn't like anybody. Given his way, he would have emptied the lantern and torched the barn before riding away. Thus far the venture had been too tame to suit him. He was angry because he had missed seeing the fight.

"Put out the light," Dalke ordered when they were ready to go. "We will head north out of the valley."

"What happened, Mr. Dalke?" a man inquired. "Did you have trouble with the Dutchman?"

"He ordered us to clear out. We'll leave by the back way. Take it easy until we're away from the buildings. The man is on a tear."

The lantern was extinguished before Hein got to the barn. He took care, expecting Dalke to set the posse on him in reprisal and take Lotus Flower by force. The departure at the rear surprised and enraged him. Cursing, he sprinted forward, pounding around the building as the riders swarmed away to the north. The creaking of leather and the movement of horses swiftly became a melee of panic as he started to work the Winchester, firing by sound, not by sight. A horse squealed. Voices clamored in consternation. Pistol flashes scored the dark. Someone roared, "Ride! *Get out of here!*"

Hein thought the shouter was Dalke and shot at the sound. Horses raced off through the night. He continued to shoot as long as he could hear. A wounded horse was threshing about on the ground. Disregarding the injured animal, he padded around to the front of the barn and went inside. A flaring match served to locate the lantern on its wire hook. He lit it and retraced his route around the walls to the rear.

The wounded horse had stopped struggling. When Hein extended the lantern at arm's length past the corner, it lifted its head, a last effort, for after that pitiful plea for succor it died. Hein's head pushed out from the corner like a wary animal peering around a rock. He saw Dean Dalke sitting against the siding, holding his head in both hands. He did not look up when Hein stepped forth, perhaps did not hear him.

Dalke's pistol holster was empty. A look at the dead horse assured Hein that Dalke's rifle was still in the scabbard. He put down the lantern as gently as if it were a soft-shelled egg, laid his rifle beside it, straightened his shoulders and marched over to

Dalke. Bending from the waist, he pulled away the covering hands.

"Now," he said, "we finish."

Dazedly Dalke looked up at the shadowed face. Almost caressingly, Hein reached for the unprotected throat.

"You shall not haff her. She iss mine."

Belatedly, Dalke struggled to rise.

"Rock of ages, cleft for me, let me hide myself in Thee."

Something like a great black bird swirled out of the night to cover the lantern, blotting out the light. There was a swish like that of a passing whirlwind as a running form slammed into Hein, knocking him into a sliding sprawl. The man hunkered against the building felt strong fingers dig into his arm. A voice whispered close and low, "Come!"

Propelled as much by the other's power as by his own, Dalke arose and followed the guiding hand around the barn to shelter from raging lead. Sitting up, Fritz Hein emptied his pistol at everything he heard or thought he heard. The shooting done, he listened, and heard nothing except the pulsing thumping in his ears.

Heaving to his feet, he moved over to look for the lantern. Searching hands touched a blanket. The light was out. Pawing further, he tried to find his rifle. It was not where he had left it. In anger, not in fear, he ran toward the house. At his going, two figures stepped from hiding near a barn wall.

"Is that you, Willows?" Dalke asked. "I heard a mouth harp."

"Get out of here, Dalke, and stay out."

"Hein killed my horse."

"There is a horse in the barn. Swap with him like I swapped with you."

Nothing more was said until they were inside the building. There Willows moved about in the dark with assurance.

"You seem to know your way around," Dalke commented.

"I've been here before. I know where he keeps his saddles. I'll saddle for you if you want. We better get a move on. I think Hein went up to re-stock."

"The men went off without me."

"Probably won't miss you until they start to count. Think they will come back?"

"Maybe. Maybe not until daylight. Who wants to face Hein's rifle in the dark?"

"Not me. Certainly not me."

"You released my wife. Where is she now?"

"She is set on finding the old woman. Mrs. Hein ain't in the house. What happened to her?"

"I don't know. Hein doesn't know. She left. Who are you, Willows? What is your interest in my wife?"

"I knew her before you did. Thought maybe you might want to sell her."

"Help me find her, Willows. I will pay you well."

"The horse is ready to go. Hit the breeze."

"You broke jail. You killed a deputy. I'm not without influence, Willows. I'll do what I can for you if—"

"You got sucked in on a frame. Either that or you're lying. I never drilled the deputy. If you hadn't set the law on me, it wouldn't have happened. Just because I knocked you on your tail—"

"You attacked me. You were on my property. All I did was ask—"

"Like I was a bum and you owned the world. I like to swing on folks like you, Mr. high-and-mighty. I was gettin' along all right with the deputy when Sid Durham came runnin' in like a stampedin' steer. Only steers don't tote guns. I saw he meant to shoot, so I drew on him. His shot hit the deputy. I should have killed Durham, only I didn't want to take on the whole town. Durham lied his head off. I never shot anybody."

"You can't prove it."

"I can if I ever get Durham alone. I'll tie his tail in knots. How much will you pay to get your wife back? A thousand? Two?"

"Do you know where she is?"

"I might find her. How much? Make it a thousand, and promise to brace Durham about the shooting."

"I don't want her soiled."

"She won't be. She is the kind of woman who turns men's heads. Do you know that? She doesn't.

Now beat it. I'll get in touch with you when the time comes. You're lucky to get out of here alive."

The voice drifted away. Lost for the moment amid uncertainties, Dalke led the horse outside, mounted and rode toward a starry W in the sky.

8

When Enright rode back to the place where he and Pinkham had spread out their bedrolls, he found them ready to be lashed to the pack on Nancy's back. As he jerked the last half-hitch tight, Pinkham called to him, "Leave the horses and come up here, Joe. We've got some action."

He looked up at the dusky figure limned above the grassy slope. Morning was edging the eastern sky rim with pale rose.

"I went down as far as the barn," Pinkham told him. "There's a dead horse down there. Dalke's."

Enright was startled. "Crawlin' crawdads! Now we've got a murder."

"Maybe. Maybe not. I heard someone in the barn. I didn't go in."

"Afraid of a horse?"

"No horse. Wrong part of the barn. Also somebody in the house. He came down to the barn a while ago. Went out through the corral and headed for the horse pasture. I think it is Hein. Somebody who knows the premises. It's getting light enough to pick him up with the glasses."

They climbed to the top of the knoll and hunkered down in the grass.

"Whoever is in the barn is keeping away from Hein." Pinkham was using the glasses. "It's him, all right. He is going along the pasture lane, carrying one of his whips."

"Going after horses on foot? With a whip? That's not smart. A rancher ought to have sense enough to keep a wrangling horse handy."

"He would have. Somebody took it. That bust-up a while ago upset his hay wagon."

"Lawdy-daw! That bunch scattered in all directions like somebody threw a stick of dynamite."

"See anything of them?"

"Not a smidgin. Seems like if anything happened to Dalke, they would come back in daylight and look around. You got any idea who is in the barn? Dalke? Willows? Maybe it is the girl."

"We can afford to wait to find out. Hein is fixin' to leave."

They took turns watching Fritz Hein through the field glasses. For half an hour he chased about on foot, trying to drive three horses into the lane that would herd them toward the open gate of the smaller corral.

"That rangy roan is the leader," Enright com-

mented. "He is driving Hein nuts. Having himself
some fun. Either that, or he is afraid of the whip.
Is Hein mean to his animals?"

"Well, no. Not usually. Maybe a kick in the belly
or a jab with a pitchfork if one gives him trouble.
Ooops—there they go. The roan finally decided to
run into the lane. Hope Hein doesn't beat out his
brains when he gets corraled. All the gates are open.
They're heading for the barn."

"Maybe the roan decided to settle for a mess of
oats. Hey, gimme those glasses. I'll be a Chinaman's
uncle! Look what's popped out behind the barn."

Pinkham took the glasses. "The redhead! She is
carrying a suitcase."

"Hiding from Hein. They have had a bust-up. Gimme another look at her. That dame is acting scared."

The woman was still there, crouched against the
siding on the north, when Hein led out two horses
and went toward the house. He had turned the third
horse into the large corral. The gate between the
two corrals was open, but he had closed the gate
to the lane.

"Pink, he saddled the roan and put a pack saddle
on the bay."

"I'm looking at him. You don't need the glasses.
It is light enough now."

"I need them to watch the redhead. She is sneakin'
along like a sore-footed Indian to peek around at
Hein. Now she is going back into the barn. Wonder

what's in the portmanteau."

"Probably the family jewels."

They watched Hein drag out a pack from the kitchen and heft it to the pack saddle.

"Planning on an extended visit," Enright observed. "Maybe he is going off to see his grandma. Do we do anything about the redhead?"

"Depends on which way Hein goes. I aim to trail him. If he comes this way, we'll have to hightail it for the timber. If he crosses the creek and goes into the foothills, we ought to have time for a word with the lady. The crew is up that way. Could be Hein has decided not to stick around here alone. We'll know more about that when we find out what happened last night. Maybe the lady can tell us. . . . Well, let's go down and mount up. He is riding toward the creek. We won't have to run."

In short order they were far enough down the knoll for the barn to conceal them from the departing Hein.

"I hope the dame isn't hostile," Enright said. "I don't want to be shot on an empty stomach. Maybe we can talk her into fixing us some breakfast."

"Not likely. Hein locked up the house. We'll live on our fat for a while until we find out where he is going."

"Well, I hope he stops before he gets to Wyoming. Lawdy-daw, the dame is coming out. She didn't fetch her case."

As they neared the barn, the woman came running, her hands outstretched. "Oh my, am I glad to
see you! I've been scared to death."

She wasn't pale, she didn't look overly scared,
and her bloom certainly placed her a long way
ahead of the old man with the scythe.

"Howdy, ma'am," Enright greeted her genially.
"Why are you out here all by yourself?"

Wary green eyes inspected him. "Such terrible
goings-on! Oh, misters, you've got to take me away
from this awful place."

Both men dismounted.

"Why did you hide from Hein?" Pinkham asked.

"I've been scared silly he would find me. I
climbed out my window last night while he was
whippin' that woman."

The change in Pinkham caused her green eyes
to flare. "What woman?" he rapped out.

"I dunno. Some Chinese. They called her Lotus."

"Where is she?"

"Lord, I dunno. That Hein man is batty in the
head. I'm not gonna stick around near him. Misters,
I've had it. I packed up my best things and climbed
out my window. Listen, I seen a side-saddle in the
barn. You men catch up that horse yonder and help
me get out of here. I know how to ride. I'm not
afraid to go off alone. Any place is better than
here."

"What is your name?" Enright inquired.

"Tillie Haworth. What's yours?"

He told her, and introduced Pinkham.

"Pleased to meecha, I'm sure. I heard them say you was lawmen."

Pinkham surmised that Tillie was not as pleased to see them as she pretended. The green eyes were experienced. They did not look scared.

"What about Lotus?" he insisted. "You said Hein whipped her. When? How long has she been here? Where is she now?"

"I dunno nothin' about her. Never seen her before in my whole life. Near as I can figure out, they caught her sneakin' around in the house last night. Hein and Dalke got into a fuss about her. Had a he— er, dickens of a fight. Scared me to death. I climbed out of my window and hid in the grass. I intended to go to the barn and ask the men to help me, but I was afraid to. Hein and Dalke was tryin' to beat each other to death. I heard a harp playin'. Some tall feller grabbed the Chinee and slung her over his shoulder."

Tillie shuddered realistically. "Gawd, I didn't know what happened, misters. Honest I don't. A while ago Hein was talkin' to himself like crazy. Goin' on about his wife, and Dalke, and somebody named Willows. He is goin' after Willows, that's what he is doin'. He aims to kill him."

"Get after him," Pinkham said to Enright. "I don't

want to lose track of him."

"Why not leave Nancy here? Trailing with a pack horse will be a handicap."

"Good idea. Lead her inside, and we'll stow the pack. Then get after Hein. I'll saddle up for Miss Haworth."

"Missus. Mr. Haworth passed away. I'm a widder woman."

When Nancy was unloaded and turned into the corral with the other horse, Enright walked on through the barn to check on Hein. "He is still in sight. I'll find a bridle and bring in Mrs. Haworth's steed."

The redhead pointed to a fringe-topped surrey standing nearby. "He brung me out here in that. If you was to hitch up both of them horses, I could get away without wearin' myself out."

"We'll have to keep our pack mare, ma'am. May I ask what you're doing here? Are you related to Hein?"

The green eyes rounded. "Gawd no! He hired me to cook for him. I don't come cheap, mister. He gimme a nice bonus."

"To take Mrs. Hein's place?"

The rather puffy eyelids narrowed. "What do you mean by that crack?"

"No offense. Where is Mrs. Hein?"

"How would I know that? I've never seen her. I come out here thinkin' I was goin' to help another woman cook and do stuff like that. Hein said his wife was gettin' puny. When I got here she was gone. He about had a fit. Right then I began to wish I hadn't listened to him. Everybody fightin'! Lawmen snoopin' around! I ain't done nothin' wrong. Not intentionally I ain't. I'm a respectable woman."

"Hein took along a pack. To me that indicates he will be gone for a spell. Yet he left a horse in the corral. Surely he must have found out you weren't in your room. He wouldn't leave without passing the word to you. What I want to know is why he didn't look for you."

"Maybe he did. I dunno. I was afraid he would. Don't ask me what he did. I tell you the man is crazy."

Enright came in with the horse. "I opened the pasture gate so Nancy can get her lunch. There is plenty of water. I better cut out now. Hein is going along pretty good. So long, ma'am. Have a nice ride."

Tillie sniffed. "'Tain't nothin' to joke about," she said to Pinkham. He was saddling the horse. It was tractable, a long-legged, wide-breasted dappled gray gelding. Tillie was eying her mount with disfavor.

"I hate to leave the rest of my things, but I s'pose I've got to. I saw Hein locking the house."

"Get your case, and I'll tie it to the saddle. I suppose your money is in it. How much did he give you?"

She eyed him warily. "Why do you want to know that?"

"Just curious. I'm sure you wouldn't make off with anything that doesn't belong to you."

She flushed. "Well, I like that! He gimme three hundred. I'm not cheap. I don' work for nothin'. Comin' way out here! I must have been out of my mind."

Or greedy, Pinkham thought. "That's a nice amount. Get the case. The horse is ready."

He wondered about her hesitation. She seemed draggy as she went to the surrey and brought out a compact leather-bound case from beneath the seat, watching closely as he secured it to the saddle on the off side. This done, he led the horse outside and helped Tillie mount. The way she sat and took over the reins showed she was no greenhorn.

"Do you know this country, Mrs. Haworth?"

"I ain't afraid. I'll find the way."

Pinkham wasn't sure about that, but it was apparent the woman was determined to leave, and he wanted to join Enright without further delay.

"You have a lot of daylight in your favor, and a good horse under you. After you get out of the valley, follow the creek until you strike a trail. Keep on it. About mid-afternoon you should come in sight of a little place called Clark. You can put up there for the night, maybe arrange to get home by tomorrow. Depends on where you live, of course."

Tillie volunteered no information about that. They parted without goodbyes. Pinkham looked back before crossing the creek. The dappled gelding was just topping the knoll. Tillie did not spare a parting glance for the Hein premises. She rode well. He was still subject to misgivings about letting her go off alone. However, he also had the feeling that, under the blooming exterior, Tillie Haworth was as hard as steel. She could take care of herself.

Enright rode out to meet him as he neared the foothills.

"Hein is following what appears to be an old drive trail. I reckon this is the way they take their stock to the benchlands."

Pinkham nodded. "About a day's drive ahead. A man on horseback can make it in less than half that time. The redhead thinks Hein is going to find Willows. Probably aims to take along a bunch of his riders. According to her, Willows carried Lotus away. Surely he wouldn't do that. She must have gone with him willingly. I wish I could be sure of that."

"Now you've got something else to fret about. She got to the ranch without us knowing anything about it. She ditched the buggy somewhere, if that's the way she came. Do you reckon Hein really whipped her?"

"The redhead was lying all over the place. She knows more than she told us. The only thing I'm sure about is that she was itchin' to get away. What

Dalke told us about Mrs. Hein must be so. Haworth said she was gone when they got to the ranch. Hein delivered the redhead in that surrey we saw in the barn. Haworth told me that Hein had a fit when he found out his wife had left. Looks like the old lady got sore and went to live with the crew."

"More to it than that, unless she didn't mean what she wrote about dying. I have a funny feeling about that message. Seems real to me, like a call from the grave. Whatever set her off wasn't a handful of peanuts. A sick woman wouldn't take off to roost with a bunch of cow waddies unless she was afraid to stay at home."

The horses had followed a coulee into a winding narrows which zigzagged between and around small hills, green outposts of the heights beyond. Pinkham lifted a precautionary hand as he sighted Hein high on a timbered slope. They watched, unmoving until he had gone from view.

Enright puffed out his cheeks and blew. "I'd hate for Whippy to get wise and lay for us in a gooseberry bush. I like to breathe through my nose, not through a hole in my chest."

"I doubt he thinks anything about being trailed. Everyone else had left the ranch. When Hein fixes his mind on something, he sticks to it like a cockleburr in a horse's tail."

"Funny about the redhead. He didn't bother to look for her."

"I imagine she is of little importance to him, less so than what he has in mind."

"That Willows keeps boogerin' me. Did he come out here because he is in a war with Hein, on account of Dalke, or to help the girl?"

"Help her or grab her. We've got to think about that."

"Yeah, I was, but I didn't want to mention it. I've got another question. I'm full of them. How come Mrs. Hein sent word to Lotus by him? I don't like that jigger. I don't cotton to black guns, black clothes or black horses. Give me some color. Anything but running red."

"You have such inspiring thoughts. I see Hein again. Take the glasses and look past that cliff top that looks like your backbone with the meat off."

"My spine is up and down, not north to south. I don't need your glass eyes. I've got the best lookers in this crowd."

"I suppose you see that gnat crawling up his back?"

"Not a gnat. It's a wooly worm. I hope you remembered to kiss the redhead goodbye for me. She is sharper than she pretends."

"Right. And no stranger to a horse. She fussed around some, but she wasn't bothered about going off alone. What do you think about that?"

"It's a long, lonesome ride. Seems kind of funny, like lots of other things about this deal. I'm downright curious. First off, I wished I had stayed at home. Now you couldn't drive me off with a skunk bag."

They talked as they rode, passing the time over the miles while the sun climbed the sky. They were hungry. They didn't want to lose Hein. So they rode.

"Man, this grass is something to rave about," Enright observed. "A cow could fill her paunch without moving out of her tracks."

"A critter won't do that unless it is powerful hungry. Acts like a kid in a candy store who wants a bite out of every jar. We used to call that peak The Devil's Finger. I've been up here lots of times, but not up there. I never had a yen to be a mountain sheep."

"Just an ordinary goat. Lordy, look at the stock out yonder! Fritz Hein is a rich man. Think of having this kind of range no more than fifteen miles from home, and the valley to boot. He can afford to be mean."

"I'd like to know how he got it. Must have had money when he first settled the valley."

"Is there a building up here?"

"A cabin. In the edge of a patch of woods. We're three or four miles south of it. There is a good spring, and a way to get in with a wagon. The men live in tents except in bad weather."

They had stopped in a swale which had the appearance of being gouged out of a gentle slope. Boulders and smaller rocks strewed the upper edge. Dead vines and green trailed over the rocks. Both men dismounted, and Pinkham went ahead to climb up amid the rocks where he could see out. Enright lifted a canteen from his saddle horn. His Adam's apple bobbed. Carrying the canteen, he went to join Pinkham.

"Want a swig? Hey, a bunch of those cow brutes are looking this way. First thing we know they will be coming over to investigate. Where is our whip boy?"

"Still headed toward that peak. When he gets to the trees, we'll cross the bench. He would spot us if we went into the open."

"Remember to ride in front of me in case he waits in the timber to look back."

They descended a crumbling dirt bank. Before mounting, both men removed their rifles from the saddle boots and made sure they were ready for action.

"An ounce of prevention is bad news for the undertaker," Enright said quizzically. "One time I forgot to look at my gun, and a snake bit me. Swelled up like a balloon."

"No wonder, seeing what he bit. Probably killed him. Did you ever see a balloon?"

"Once. Some French dude at a fair. Heard later some drunk thought it was a big bird comin' to get him and shot it down."

"Hope he didn't nail the Frenchman. Let's go. Time to move."

Their horses were soon pounding across the grass-land toward the borderline trees.

"The sun is starting to bear down," Enright said to his partner. "It's nice we've got some cool air. Good for my complexion."

"It must get pretty warm up on The Devil's Finger."

"Give a crow a hotfoot. Nothing up there but naked rock."

9

Faith Hein knew she did not have long to live. For some time she had been unable to work in a stooping position, nor could she mount upon a chair and reach to a cupboard top. There were moments in the stillness of night when her heart fluttered in her breast like a trapped bird struggling to break free, and she would awaken, fighting for breath. The sickness that followed seemed to sway her bed gently like a craft bobbing upon the waves.

She sat alone on a barren hilltop beside a cairn of stones, legs folded, dark-veined hands resting in her lap. The rocky arete formed a tonsure above the timber line a hundred feet below. The day was young. The morning sun had not yet warmed the winds. Shivering, Faith crossed her arms on the front of her short coat, hugging her frail body, trembled by her thoughts rather than by the coolness of the mountain air. She had come adequately dressed. The horse she had ridden stood below, tethered amid stubby-branched trees. Nearby, her small pack lay open to the sun. The horse had been grazed during the night and watered in the morning.

There was no marker for the grave. After her arduous climb to the summit, Faith had knelt on knobby knees to pray. Dull-eyed, she gazed out across a green sea of timber and sweeping benchlands. With the worsening of her malady, her sight had failed. The distance was veiled in haze.

On the benchlands cattle by the thousands browsed or lay surfeited, chewing their cuds. Run-off and seepage from the heights abundantly watered the grasslands, provided drink for livestock and the few humans there to watch over them. Snow lingered on the less exposed slopes and sierras.

Faith could not see the cattle or the men, their chuck wagons or their tents. And though their vision was much better than hers, they could not see her. Neither were they aware of her presence. As far as she knew, she and Fritz were the only persons around who knew about the grave. The men who had helped bury Gustave were dead, or long gone from the ranch. Gustave had been her only love, save for the girl who had come late into her life.

"Faith, mit the girl gone you candt keep up your vork. I bring in anodder voman."

"You make me afraid for Lotus. I see how you look at her."

"She iss not your Lotus. She iss Dalke's Lotus. Dalke giff me a t'ousand dollar. I pay von hunnert.

I gedt me a vomen for less dan dot."

"She *is* mine Lotus. I luff her like mine own childt."

Faith was not at the ranch to witness the arrival of Tillie Haworth. When Hein drove up to the house with the buxom redhead, esconced amid her baggage and furbelows in a fringe-topped surrey, and called to Faith to come forth, she was not there. The house where she had labored for so long was deserted. At once the newcomer, lured by promises, evidences of affluence and cash in hand, witnessed a display of Hein temper. On the whole, however, Tillie preferred not having another woman around. In fact, she thought she glimpsed opportunity through an unexpectedly opened door. Men were men. She was a good cook and, she believed, well endowed with other attractions.

Hein had told her he had a sick wife. He looked healthy enough. Indeed, he seemed vital and very sure of himself. Besides, he owned the place!

Faith Hartmann, the bride of young Gustave Ludwig von Gluck, had come to settle in the "Golden West." He had money to do as he wished—buy land, hire help, build his valley citadel. So they had come to reside in comfort on the frontier, Gustave, Faith, and Gustave's first cousin, Fritz Hein. Fritz was the one with the business head. He managed everything but the personal affairs of the newly-

weds, and they were content to have it so. Gustave
trusted his cousin completely. . . .

Belatedly, Faith was thinking about the horse.
She did not want to leave it tethered, saddled, perhaps to be deprived of food and water or to fall
prey to some beast. Driving herself, she slowly descended to the timber. The gentle old horse pricked
its ears and nickered softly at her coming. She patted
the star in the bay head, loosened the girth and
dragged off the saddle, letting it lie, then led the
horse nearer to the grassland before slipping off the
bridle. The bay did not want to leave. She caressed
him again and turned away.

"Go, Reddy, go! *Auf wiedersehen,* olt friend."

Reddy remained standing until she went out of
sight toward the monument rock. Accepting his dismissal, he started to graze.

Faith was exhausted when she reached the cairn
again. She lay for a while, face to the cloudless sky,
then sat up to ease the laboring of her heart, opening her mouth to suck in breath. She reached over
to take up a small metal box. The lid bore the crest
of Gustave's family. Resting the box on her lap,
she opened the lid. It was not locked. The key had
been lost years before.

"Indians! Renegades! We're being raided!"

There was a terrifying awakening. Gustave had
been slain while fighting for his property. Fritz Hein

had defended his cousins against their foes. So she had believed.

Through the brief fury she had never once caught sight of a foe. When she awoke, Gustave was gone from his side of the bed. As she ran from the room, someone had yelled at her to go back and stay out of the way. She had obeyed, and in her fear had tried to block the door with furnishings from the room. Minutes later she wished she had been slain.

"Lieber Gott, Gustave ist dead!"

There had been days in limbo during which she had prayed to die. But her healthy young body had decreed otherwise. And there was Fritz. Gustave had been the gentleman, Fritz the manager of their business. He knew what to do. Faith was almost totally unfamiliar with ranch affairs. She entrusted everything to Fritz.

A year after Gustave's killing she married Fritz Hein, not because she cared for him, but because it seemed to her she had no other choice. Gustave's family had never accepted her, the daughter of a former servant woman. She knew they had been happy to load Gustave with money when he expressed a desire to make his home in America's "Wild West." She was no longer an embarrassment. Certainly she could not go back to them, or to her own people. So Hein became the nobleman, fulfilling his heart's desire, and Faith in time reverted to peasant status.

It was Fritz's custom to round up cattle and drive them to the valley at calf-branding time. He preferred this method to traveling about with a chuck wagon and setting up camps away from home. Though he did not require Faith to travel about with the crew, he had gradually assigned her to take care of them while they were at the ranch, in time constructing a bunkhouse addition to the kitchen. He trained her to accept what he believed to be the tradition of her birth and the lot of her sex. If he had wanted a lady, he would not have married Faith. He wanted a servant, and when Fritz Hein wanted something, he usually got it.

The events which led to the occasion which finished breaking Faith's heart were initiated while Hein and three men of the work force were off on a buying trip in search of new breeding blood. She did not suspect that the tall, silent-walking man had timed his visit to coincide with Hein's absence. Visitors were rare. No one came to see her. This visitor did. The novelty of the occasion and her impressions of the man stirred Faith out of a habitual withdrawal which had the appearance of complete indifference. She was skilfully led to speak of thoughts and experiences about which she had talked to no one except the girl who had won her devotion.

Lotus was nineteen when the tall dark man first came. For a while Faith had believed that his subsequent visits were due to his interest in the girl.

She was partly right. Willows was definitely attracted, but his target was Fritz Hein. He wanted the girl, he was not too inimical to mankind to feel a stirring of sympathy for the woman who had spent a considerable portion of her life in virtual servitude, but first and foremost he had come there on account of Fritz Hein.

Faith had told Lotus about the raid and the killing of her first husband, a tale of the long ago. Being an intelligent person, Lotus was aware that Faith was being led by the visitor, but saw no harm in it. In fact, she was pleased to see the woman sufficiently relaxed to talk with someone other than herself. Though somewhat disturbed by the further awareness that Willows' questions indicated a familiarity with Hein's affairs improbable in a stranger, Lotus did not discourage Faith's revelations when she recounted the events of her terrible night.

Willows came, and came again. He made no overtures to Lotus, was never alone with the girl. Her heart was elsewhere, as Faith well knew. She clung to her hopes for Lotus and Pinkham. To her he was still "the fair-haired boy."

Recognizing Willows' desires, Lotus had on one occasion stated with seeming lightness, "Mr. Hein owns this person. I could not trade myself, give myself away or run away. I think he intends to bring in another Chinese and raise for himself a herd of slaves."

Lightning struck on the day Willows came to the ranch and was told by the despairing Faith that Lotus had gone away with Dean Dalke.

"He coom much. First time he make deal for bools. Ziss time he take Lotus. She go to be fine lady. Ah-e-e-e, but I miss her zo. . . ."

Beyond a few terse questions, Willows did little talking. Nor did he linger to listen to her complaints. He wanted to be by himself. But when Hein rode in and left his horse at the barn to be cared for by the crew, Willows was waiting. The two men came to the house together, Hein walking in stiff silence, Willows stalking two paces to the rear.

Hein thrust into the kitchen, ignoring Faith, who was preparing the evening meal.

"Come!" he flung over a shoulder to the man behind, and marched into the passageway, Willows following with that odd pantherish walk. Willows did not look at Faith. His profile was chiseled stone.

Faith put down the utensil in her hand to move two steaming kettles to the rear of the wood-burning stove. She checked on a huge roast cooking in the oven, then went into the passageway, wiping her hands on the apron tied about her waist. Hein and Willows were going into the cellar room!

Faith had never seen the inside of Hein's arsenal. He always carried the keys. She had, however, explored the cellar room. But she had never gone there since Hein's trouble with the Pinkham boy. She knew

about Fritz and his whips. Men were brawling creatures who liked to wallow in blood and took pleasure in hurting. She shunned the room as if it were
a resort of the devil, in whom she firmly believed.
Fritz had never abused her save with his tongue,
but she was never without the feeling that some day
he might use a whip.

She stole along the passageway to the cellar room
door, which had been closed after Hein lighted a
lamp. Timorously, she pressed an ear to the door.
In a few minutes she was wishing she had stayed
in the kitchen. Far less painful to have gone to her
grave in ignorance!

Willows was speaking of dark deeds about which
there was no proof. Bludgeoned, Faith crept back
to the kitchen. A lost creature, she looked about like
a trapped animal with no place to go, no place to
turn. Her stunned gaze settled on a cabinet drawer.
She opened it, took out a stub pencil and a square
of paper. Placing the paper on the cabinet top, she
scribbled a message, partly in her German script,
partly in misspelled English. Folding the paper into
a strip, she wrote on the back, "LOTIS. PLESE."

Turning to more familiar tasks, she fiddled with
her cooking. Part of her mind listened for conflict
in the cellar room. Instead, footsteps sounded in the
passageway. Hein marched through the kitchen. His
eyes were pits of fury. He did not look at Faith.
Behind him stalked Willows, the big black-handled

pistol still in its holster.

Moving with a swiftness that surprised Willows, she thrust the paper into his hand. He saw Lotus' name, gave Faith a searching glance, nodded and rammed the paper into a pocket. Almost fainting in her relief, she sank into a chair. Two great tear-drops oozed from her eyes to tumble down her thin cheeks. She fumbled for the corner of her apron.

Willows spoke outside the kitchen door. "Go with me halfway to the barn. Stay put until I'm out of gunshot range, or I'll kill you."

Before Willows' horse topped the knoll, Hein had entered the barn. Presently he rode away without telling anyone where he was going. Lying sleepless that night, Faith heard him go into his room after midnight!

Willows had accused Hein of brutally whipping a man who had come to the ranch. The accusation was the prelude of a horrid, heart-rending tale, a revelation that shattered the listening woman.

"Years ago you paid Pete Anderson five hundred to stage a fake raid on this place. That much dough was a gold mine to Pete and me, a pair of young hellers looking for easy money and a good time, usually broke. We had a ball. We thought it was a big joke on some visiting dude from across the big pond. That's what you told Pete. We didn't do any damage except fire some hay shocks out away from the cattle sheds. We hollered and whooped and burned powder. You suckered us into helping cover up a murder. Neither one of us set foot inside this house."

No denials, no protests from the accused; only a grim silence.

"That money spoiled us, Hein. Easy stuff. We wanted more. We got caught trying to clean out a bank. The law dogs sent us up for twenty years. Taught us something. Don't get caught. When we heard about that other Dutchman getting killed in a raid, we knew we'd been played for suckers. While we broke rocks, you got rich. You glommed onto the Dutchman's woman and everything else he had. Oh, we did a lot of thinking about you, *Mister* Hein. Pete rode in for a little confab about money. You skinned him with a whip, stuffed a hundred into his pocket and told him to get lost. A lousy hundred bucks! Pete lost the sight in his left eye. Up to then I only wanted money, *Mister* Hein. Now I am gonna mix in some blood. *I have got you over a barrel.*"

Faith sat looking down into the metal box. Money, hoarded by dribs through the years. Gustave's wedding ring, which no longer fitted her gnarled fingers. A certificate printed in German. A leaf cut from her Bible, bearing family records from Hesse-Darmstadt. A crumbling flower pressed between two pieces of yellowed cardboard.

She closed the box and scooted closer to the stones. Slowly, with difficulty, she moved enough stones away to make room for the box, then restored them, patiently fitting them until satisfied. She patted the stones.

"Lieber Gustave. . . . Ich kommt. . . . Ich kommt."

Idly she noticed blood at the tip of a finger, a torn fingernail, and touched it with a pale tongue. She sat, head bowed, her eyes closed. After a while she lay back on the level beside the cairn, her legs stretched out, the old boots side by side. Some minutes later she removed the scarf that bound her hair and laid it across her brow to protect her eyes from the sun. The worn hands were folded upon her breast.

Presently Lotus Flower came over to sit beside her and hold her hand. The thin mouth softened in a smile.

Such a lovely child. . . .

"Do not vorry, Gustave. Fritz didt not win."

10

Fritz Hein climbed the shady side of the monument rock. As he neared the summit, the sun reached around to heat the hard skin of Devil's Finger. The wind had turned warm, lapping at his sweat. There was no trail up the finger, animal or human, but there were crumblings, scratchings, displaced small rocks which signified that someone had climbed before him.

He was thinking about Faith and her bitter talk, mumblings about dying, being buried beside her dear Gustave. Dear Gustave! He didn't care how she felt about Gustave. He did care about her leaving the ranch in mulishness over his bringing in another woman.

Faith's sense of direction was so poor that she had never gone far from the buildings alone. A dozen years ago he had refused to accompany her to the grave any more, though he permitted her to make the journey if one of the men went along. She had never allowed her escort to climb to the summit.

The grave was her shrine, to which she desired to go alone.

She had been pretty in her youth, a big girl in full bloom, exciting to his senses, but a peasant. Gustave had married below his station. Hein had long believed that the family was relieved when Gustave "went west" across the Atlantic. They preferred providing the necessary money to accepting his peasant wife.

As the years passed, Faith had retreated more and more within herself. Hein didn't mind that. His reason for marriage had not been affection. She satisfied him until he tired of her. Now he thought of her as sullen and ugly. However, this didn't bother him, as long as she did her work.

When he arrived at the ranch in company with Tillie Haworth and found an empty house, he had been furious. He assumed she had gone to the benchland to stay with the men. They would welcome her, of course. Thor Jansson was a good everyday cook, but no match for Faith. . . .

A strange feeling came over him as he neared the summit. Had she really believed she was near death? Can anyone name the time of death unless by one's own hand? Surely she would not—

Hein was not used to uneasiness. He was angry with himself because he had come to Devil's Finger first, before going on to the benchland cow camp. Had Faith made a believer of him?

"I vill go up to mine Gustave. He is the one who luffs me."

"Gustave is by der vorms."

"I know v'y you vant anodder voman. I vill not shtay here."

"Ach shod opp. Long ago I giff up mine bedt to you."

"So you could fill it mit Lotus. I know vot you mean to do."

"Vot differcnce to you? You no good for me no more."

"Hah! You kill my Gustave to get me."

That swine Willows. Of course she had listened outside the door. Willows had been nothing but trouble, trouble, trouble.

This was not the first time Hein had run against the impenetrable wall of his wife's stubborn will. Some months after purchasing Lotus, he had awakened to find his light burning. Faith was sitting beside him on the bed. When he attempted to rise, he felt the sharp edge of a butcher knife against his throat.

Faith told him grimly, speaking in German, that if he ever violated the girl, she would kill him while he slept. As the shock of awakening abated, he considered her with sardonic amusement; in fact, with grudging admiration. At that time Lotus was "the liddle Chinee." The warning meant nothing. However, as Lotus developed into womanhood, the situation changed. He was not afraid of anything Faith might do, never had been. In his own way, as far as he was able, he felt affection for the girl and had conducted himself with restraint. Although Dalke's infatuation came as a sort of irritation, it also provided relief. Dalke took Lotus away when the sight of her would no longer fill his thoughts. Furthermore, Hein had taken advantage of Dalke's desire to make a handsome profit. He had learned, however, that Lotus' absence did not put a stop to thought! Dalke. Dalke and Lotus Flower. The thoughts had become torture.

He climbed Devil's Finger, his mind a jumble.

This was Faith's preserve. He was ready to invade her shrine. He topped the eminence like a wary animal, poking his head above the rim. Faith lay supine beside the cairn.

"Faith?"

He stood high in a world filled with silence. Strange emotions stirred. He was warm from climbing. Most certainly there was no chill in the air. The grave did that to him, and the woman lying there.

He reared up into full view and removed the rifle slung about his shoulders, laying it upon bare rock thrust up from the foundations of the earth. Once again he spoke his wife's name. She did not answer; she did not move.

Swiftly he crossed and stooped beside her. Thin

hands were folded laxly on her breast, her legs neatly disposed. He shook her firmly, oddly gentle, then bent to lay an ear above her heart. Faith had indeed come there to die.

He sat back on his heels, staring at the tired face, the sagging chin, the hollow cheeks. She was no more attractive in death than she had been in life.

He laid aside the cap he wore outdoors in preference to a hat, took off his gunbelt and the shoulder holster, removed his shirt. The bowie had been left below. The humps of muscle on his shoulders, the swelling biceps, the strong torso attested to a strength beyond that of the average man. He started to disassemble the cairn rock by rock.

Before reaching whatever remained of his dead cousin, he came upon his wife's keep-sake box. Having never seen it before, he wondered where she had kept it hidden. Crouching, he opened the lid.

The money surprised him. He removed it, laying it beside his shirt. Junk. A woman's fluff, he thought until, reversing the marriage certificate, he saw writing on the back. He read the German script.

"My Lotus, I waited. You did not come. Your man stopped you. I know. I came here to hide from Fritz. He killed my husband Gustave. *Herr* Willows knows."

Bunching the papers pawed from the box, Hein

tore them to shreds, to be flung from the air into the mountain wind. In a spasm of rage, he leaped upon the box, stamped it into a shapeless mass of tin and threw it after the scattered papers. The violent action seemed to calm him. He resumed dismantling the cairn and saw at last what was left of the man he had slain: bones in the tatters of a uniform, lying in ghoulish dignity, the skull tipped forward, with grinning teeth and holes for eyes.

Hein pulled Faith over beside the raggedy skeleton, rearranged her clothing and her hands, then labored to rebuild the cairn, a little wider, a little flatter than before. There were stones enough. He was sweaty, dirty, and out of sorts when the job was done.

Moving over beside his discarded possessions, he took up the undershirt to use as a towel, dabbing at the doeskin pants, swabbing away running sweat. The undershirt was not sufficient. Scowling, he impatiently took up the shirt. He wiped and wiped, ending by dusting off his highly polished boots. Rifle slung at his back, he went to the rim where he had mounted and threw the ruined garments down the peak side.

Muttering to himself, he climbed down the monument rock.

11

"Now you've got me climbing mountains," Enright grumbled, wiping away sweat. "Least you could have done was pick rocks in the shade."

He knew very well why they were climbing in the sun: to avoid discovery by the descending Fritz Hein. They had waited until he showed over the rim before circling to begin their climb.

"What the devil do you suppose he was doing up on this eagle roost?"

"Hunting bird's eggs," Pinkham declared solemnly. "That's why, I'm going up: to see if there are any left."

"We should have hung around and arrested him when he came down."

"Arrested him for what?"

"For being alive. That's a crime in his case."

"These rocks are hotter than a bowl of chili."

Enright was the first over the rim. "Crawling crawdads! Look at that!"

Pinkham climbed over into sight of the cairn

of stones. His glance studied the stones as he moved on past to the opposite rim to use his field glasses.

Enright stopped at the cairn. "So this is what the whipper did with her. He left her here and came back to bury her. I'm going to enjoy putting the cuffs on that man."

"Those rocks have been here a long time, Joe. He moved them around."

Enright was peeling off his shirt. "If you're going to make a grave robber out of me, you've got to help. I'll share with you fifty-fifty."

"Hein is down there by the trees, kicking some stuff around. He is half naked. There's a saddle among the stuff."

Pinkham came back and started to get rid of equipment and his upper clothing. Enright had attacked the rock pile.

"Heck, Pink, I think we've found the family grave-yard. If a man wanted to hide a body, surely he wouldn't need to bring it way up here. Did the Heins ever have any children?"

Pinkham started to work. "Never heard of any. Go take a look at Hein. I don't want to lose him."

While Enright was using the glasses, Pinkham called out words that brought him back to the cairn. "Here she is, Joe, waiting for the rats and worms under two feet of stone. She is not alone."

"Bones!" Enright exclaimed. "Rags and bones."

They uncovered the skeleton.

"Good Lord, Pink, it was a man. His skull was split open."

"Happened a long time ago. Must have been kin to her."

"That's why Hein brought her here?"

"Or why she came. Joe, feel her legs. They're getting stiff. Her hands are still limber. I can't find a mark on her. She wasn't shot. She wasn't choked. I think she came here to die. Hein just found her a while ago and buried her. If he had killed her, the body would still be warm, and if he had brought her here a while back, rigor wouldn't be just setting in."

"Then she came here on account of this soldier boy."

"If he was a soldier. Could have been some kind of ceremonial uniform. Well, let's put back the rocks. I'll take another look at Hein."

He was soon back at work. "He cleared out that stuff down there. Carried it and the saddle into the woods. Now he has unloaded his own pack and opened it. He's putting on a dry shirt. I'll bet this was the hardest work he has done in a long time. He doesn't like to get dirty."

"What do we do next? According to you, he didn't do anything to his wife but bury her. Nobody is going to fault him for that, especially since we have had a look at the body."

"He didn't fix up a pack horse just to come here. I don't know why he came. I don't know if he expected to find her here. She may have told him where she was coming. I'm guessing that he didn't expect to find her dead. I want to talk to him, but first I'd like to find out where he is going. If, as I believe, he intends to track down Willows and Lotus Flower, I want to get there first. Willows just might underestimate him. I'll never do that. He is as deadly as a rattlesnake."

"But you can't stomp him because he might bite someone, arrest him on account of bad intentions."

"It's our business to prevent crime as well as to catch lawbreakers. Well, these poor souls are covered up again. Let's leave them in peace. What we need now is a big towel."

"I'm going to carry my duds until we get down to the horses. Pink, dang it, I wish we had a Bible. I hate just to pile rocks on the lady's face and go off and leave her. She is going to spend a long time alone. I learned the 23rd Psalm when I was a kid. Do you know it?"

"Maybe. I can try. Doesn't seem that the Lord did much for her when she was alive. No harm asking Him to take over now."

They stood shoulder to shoulder beside the re-made cairn, their heads bowed. "The Lord is my shepherd, I shall not want. . . ."

When they finished, Joe Enright's eyes were moist.

"Dang it, I feel sorry for the poor woman. If I never do anything else in this world, I'm gonna find out what happened. I'll never be content until I know."

"Yeah," Pinkham agreed gruffly. "I second the motion."

He touched Enright on the shoulder and went over to take up his shirt, tying the sleeves about his waist.

12

Hein's men were stationed below a stand of blue spruce where a spring gushed from beneath mossy, stratified rock which bulged boldly from a great ridge. Water rippled from beneath a ledge higher than a man, forming a wide, shallow stream. A thousand yards or so below the place of issue, a rock dam had been laid across the stream to form a large watering pool. No spillway was needed. Spillage ran over and through the rocks of the dam.

Two saddled horses lolled within a rope "hold." Others, hobbled, were elsewhere on graze. Near a sprawling tent, the tongue of a chuck wagon had been propped up by a forked stick. Tarpaulin flies helped protect the tent from sun heat and storm. The tailgate of a supply wagon edged into the open rear of the tent.

A lean hairpin of a man and a shorter version were busy clearing away after the noon meal when

Fritz Hein approached his summer headquarters. The cook's gauntness made him look taller than he was. Bert Parker, his helper, was much younger, equally thin, and his lively dark eyes seemed too intelligent for a man in a flunky's job. None of the other men could stand Thor Jansson as a steady diet, so Hein paid Parker extra, and he stayed on the job. Oddly, or so it seemed to the others, Jansson liked him.

Parker was the first to sight the boss.

"Heiney has brought a pack horse. Maybe he is going to stay with us for a spell. I was all set for a good summer."

His quick eyes noted that a tic started to jump at the corner of Jansson's left eye. It always did that when the Swede was uneasy.

"If he gets on us about the woman, be careful what you say."

"Shucks, he has no call to blame us. We didn't invite her to come, and we couldn't send her away. She works herself to death. Sure needed that spell of rest."

In his measured, lilting tenor Jansson allowed that Mrs. Hein looked "vorse" when she left than when she came. Yellow as a pumpkin.

He shook his head, causing a straw-colored forelock to dangle over an eye. "She is a sick woman. Had no business starting off home alone. But she didn't want anyone to go along. Mind what I said: if the boss jumps us, keep your mouth shut. I've known him for fifteen years. We get along."

"Why do you? That's what I wonder. If he ever got on me, I'd bust him, then run for my life."

He laughed, appreciating himself. Jansson knew it was just talk. Abandoning their work, the two men side by side, watching Hein dismount and ground the reins.

"He aimed to get here after the men had et and gone," Parker muttered. "Depend on him for that. Howdy, Mr. Hein. What brings you up this way?"

Hein did not answer. Neither did he return the greeting.

"Thor, haff you seen *Frau* Hein?"

Jansson was not sufficiently phlegmatic to restrain a start.

"Sure. Sure. She left here yesterday morning. Said she was goin' home. Didn't she say so, Bert?"

The helper nodded. He was not too homely for a mother's love, or important enough, in Hein's opinion, to be of use in the present circumstances.

"Go find someding to do, Parker," the boss ordered curtly. "I vant to speagk mit Thor alone."

Parker shrugged. Rather than being offended by the abrupt dismissal, he was thankful to get away. Jansson had been around for a long time. He ought to know how to deal with Hein.

Parker went over to the hold, let down a rope and led one of the saddled animals outside. He mounted loosely, as if about to fall apart, and rode away slouched in the saddle as if merged with the horse. Parker had been thoroughly dried out by a thousand suns. However, he was not frail or in danger of being blown away.

"You want a steak?" Jansson asked uneasily. "I got fresh beef in the meat box up under the spring."

Hein hesitated, then acquiesced. He led the horses to water, then back to tether them at wagon wheels, standing apart. He loosened the girth of the roan and went to the stream to wash. Meanwhile, Jansson had stoked up the fire in a four-lidded stove at the rear of the tent and headed upstream, butcher knife in hand. A metal stovepipe elbowed out of the open-ended tent to extend upward a dozen feet. It was braced by wires slanting down to ground stakes. During foul weather, the stove was carried into a cabin in the timber, the pipe vented into a stone chimney. Although nearby, the cabin was not visible from the camp site.

Jansson dumped a generous spoonful of lard into a frying pan. When it started to sizzle, he slapped in a thick slice of red meat rimmed by a layer of fat. He put four left-over biscuits into the oven to warm, leaving the door open, shoved a large coffeepot nearer the firebox, and was mixing water and flour and making gravy when Hein came into the tent.

Jansson had taken note of the rifle in the saddle boot, the belted pistol, and the shoulder holster strapped around Hein's shirt. The boss usually wore a sidearm when he left the ranch premises, but the cook had never seen him so heavily armed as at present. The abundance of materials for conflict did nothing to diminish Jansson's uneasiness. He was expecting a reprimand. He hoped the juicy steak would make for better human relations. As he tended the frying meat, he kept a close watch on the biscuits. They had been unusually light and tasty. Covered with good meat gravy, they just might please a finicky boss who preferred his wife's cooking to chuck-wagon fare.

Hein sat on an upended crate. "How long did she shtay?" he asked, as if there had been no gap in their talk.

"Six or eight days, something like that. Mr. Hein, didn't your wife come home?"

"She cook for you, Thor?"

"Some. Yeah, she helped some. Stayed in the cabin mostly. We never bothered her 'cept when it rained and we had to move the stove inside."

He transferred the meat to another pan to keep it warm and dumped the gravy mixture into the frying fat, sprinkling salt as he stirred.

"She seemed mighty peaky, Mr. Hein."

"Did she ask you to tell me she vass here?"

The stirring faltered. "No, by 'tunder. Why would she ask me that?"

He didn't like Hein's staring eyes.

"One rare steak comin' up. You want to eat where you are or move out to the chuck wagon?"

Hein changed the crate to its side in order to make room for a tin plate and cup beside him.

"You want sweetenin' for your coffee?"

"Nein. Thor, you vork for me a long time. You remember that man Pingham?"

Jansson fingers an ear as if to stir his memory.

"Yeah. The young faller. The foreman said you shot him."

"Kinney tolt you that?"

"Yeah. Well, not me. I didn't ask him nothin'. Heard him mention it to somebody. Don't remember who."

Hein was wolfing the food as if he liked it. He was hungry.

"You say *Frau* Hein vass bad sick?"

"I didn't say bad. She was peaky. She got around, but she shore looked puny. I tried to get her to let one of the boys go home with her, make sure she got there all right. She wouldn't listen. Nothin' I could do about that. I couldn't tell her what to do."

"Ach, so? Vot she say venn she go?"

"Said she was goin' home. That's exactly what she said. "I go home now." And then *auf* veeder' something."

"Vot you call the big peagk to the vest? Devil Finger?"

"Some do. I don't call it anything. Good-for-nothing place."

"*Frau* Hein iss op there, dead. Climb too much for her. Killed her."

Emotions charged across Jansson's features—surprise, dismay, recurring apprehension. "T'under in heaven! She killed herself?"

Hein nodded. His glance never left the cook as he drained the coffee tin and placed it in the empty plate. Instinctively Jansson moved toward the stove.

"*Nein.* No more. Grave op there, Thor. Her first husban'. She vant to die there. She god her vish. You tell the men. I go now."

"You—you left her up there?" Jansson stammered.

The strange eyes bulged at him. "Somet'ing wrong mit dot?"

"But— What— T'under, no! Don't s'pose so. You ain't gonna have no funeral? Nothing like that?"

Hein surprised him by smiling.

"Op there on der mountain? Ve gedt a hurst, yess? Mit v'ite horses?"

"Something will get her," Jansson protested weakly.

"You care about dot? You think I don't care, yeah?"

"Sure I care. Poor old woman!"

"You think she vass olt? Maybe I not goot to her, so? Maybe she vork too hardt?"

"Look, Mr. Hein," the cook said desperately, unable to stop his floundering plunge, "it's none of my business. I just thought—"

"I already do the thinking. I coffer her mit rock. She iss vere she vants to be. I say a prayer. You go op say a prayer, Thor?"

"Sure. I never been up there. Didn't know nothin' about a grave. Didn't know she was married before. Me and the boys will go. Sure, Mr. Hein. We can find some flowers higher up. Maybe she would like that. You think she would?"

"You talk about her sometimes mit the men?"

"*No sir.* Hardly ever. I'm shore mighty sorry about the poor lady. Lucky you knew where to look for her. Don't that beat all, going up there to visit her husband's grave and dyin' on the spot? Maybe that's how the Good Father meant it to be. One never knows."

"How you think I know v'ere to look for her?"

Jansson had seen something out on the grassland that might offer a way of escape. "Bert is coming back. It's about time! I need that faller to help finish cleaning up this mess. You ready to leave? I'll help with the horses."

Hein had turned to look toward the approaching horseman. He stood for a moment, head down, looking aslant at the cook, who busied himself collecting the used utensils in a large dishpan. As if thrusting into motion, Hein went out to the horses, untied them and rode away without saying anything more. The tall cook sank upon the crate and put his face in hiding between two long-fingered hands. A quiver shook him from head to boots.

He was working when Parker put his horse away. Jansson crossly assaulted the younger man when Parker entered the tent.

"Man, he must have worked you over," Parker opined without offense. "You're crosser than a sore-tailed bear."

Jansson swore. Actually, Hein was the target, not Bert Parker. but Parker was the one who got hit. "The old woman is dead," he informed Parker. "That so-and-so covered her with rocks upon that finger mountain. Too mean to put her in a coffin. Did you know she was married before?"

"So what? A lot of them are."

"Her first man is buried up there. So Hein said. What a God-awful place to have a graveyard. Parker, you give me two bits, and you can have this job."

"Make me an offer later in the day. Right now I wouldn't take it if you gave me two bits. A couple of riders are headed this way. That's what I intended to tell the boss. Well, nuts to him. I don't aim to go lamming after him. What did he have to tell you that he didn't want me to hear? I'm downright hurt."

"What fallers?"

"I don't know whether they're fallers or faller-esses. I don't see faces too good a couple of miles away."

"By t'under, I don't cook no more. I don't care

if it's the Prasident of the United States."

"Or the Governor of Texas," Parker added, display-
ing his impudent grin. Whereupon Jansson put away
the butcher knife as if resisting temptation.

13

Obeying Dalke's startled command, the posse riders fled up the knoll away from the shooter in the dark. There was some reactive pistol fire, but no one was disposed to face about and risk expending ammunition on an unseen target. Neither did they linger to question, but when they were safe beyond the knoll they began to rattle with the liveliness of pebbles in a shaken lottery box.

"Why did he cut loose at us, Mr. Dalke?"

Dalke was not present to answer. The discovery of his absence slowed them down. Sid Durham checked them by name. There was a man for every name save one. Something had happened to Dean Dalke.

"We gotta go back!"

Durham squelched the man who had spoken. "Can you see in the dark? Think you can go back there and smell him out without getting shot?"

"Maybe he is hurt."

"Maybe he is dead. How you gonna find out? How do we know our horses ain't hurt unless we get where we can take a look? I'm gonna ride on to that place where the creek leaves the valley. If you yahoos want to go rammin' back there to eat lead, go ahead. I'm gonna wait until morning."

They came up with more questions, but Durham yelled them down. He wasn't giving up on Dalke. It wouldn't do Dalke any good to go back and get shot. "We couldn't even see the barn, let alone find a man. If Dalke is dead, nobody can help it now. But I'm goin' back in the morning. I'm gonna find out who done that shootin' and give him a belly full of lead."

The sentiment satisfied them, as did Durham's determination to wait for daylight. They rode to the designated place, dismounted, and the man who carried the camp lantern and their few utensils in a gunny bag atop his blanket pad made a light in order to inspect the horses. None of them were injured.

Durham posted a sentinel in the darkness to the south. The rest of the party had not yet settled down when the man warned them of the approach of a horse from the direction of the ranch.

"He ain't trying to be quiet. I hope it's Dalke."

Durham blew out the light, whereupon the sentinel lifted his voice.

"Hey, Sid, I think I heard someone holler when the light went out."

"Line out across the gap," Durham ordered. "Start in a bunch, and one may drop off every ten steps. We'll seal the gap. Hurry it! No shootin' unless I say so."

"Hey, Sid," the sentinel called worriedly. "I'm not gonna stay out here and let them guys salivate me."

"Well, come on in, dumbbell," Durham ordered testily. "You've done your duty."

"He slowed down," the sentinel informed him when he joined Durham. "Hear that? He is hollerin' again."

The unseen rider called, "I'm Dean Dalke. I saw your light."

The pleased sentinel yelled, "Come on in. It's us, Mr. Dalke. I'll light the lantern."

"Keep your bazoo shut!" Durham ordered angrily. "It ain't Dalke just because he says so."

He shouted, his voice shrilling rather than increasing in power. "Stop where you are! Give us a password or somethin'."

"Who in Sam Hill gave him a password?" the sentinel asked.

Durham swore at him. "Dalke, how do I know Hein ain't holdin' a gun on you?"

"Because I'm alive. Hold your fire, men. I'm

coming in. Hein killed my horse. I stole the one that was left in the barn. I am all alone out here. It's about all I can do to stick in the saddle."

"Come in slow," Durham directed, bound to have the last word. "We've got our guns pointed at you. If you ain't Dalke, you're gonna be sorry."

"I couldn't believe you men would go off and leave me," Dalke said when his horse came up to them.

They surrounded the horse and helped him alight. Durham lit the lantern. "What was Hein doing while you stole his horse?"

"I was too busy to inquire."

Dalke was looking about for a place to sit amid the scattered gear on the ground. "I'm so stiff and sore all over it gets harder and harder to move. I'm thankful we don't have to leave here early in the morning. No one will bother us here."

"Huh!" Durham disparaged. "Hein ain't gonna try any one-man expedition. I reckon he got sore at you and blew off at the rest of us. Well, he ain't gonna get away with it. I don't aim to go back to town and tell my boss I never done anything about it. Me and the boys aim to go back in the mornin' and teach the Dutchman a lesson."

Which was not precisely true, but when no one obected Durham was sufficiently heartened to assert, "From now on I'm givin' the orders. If you don't want to go back with us, you can wait here or head for home."

Dalke stared at the ground. "Whatever you say, Sid. I haven't done very well so far. What I do will depend on how I feel in the morning. I do believe you have grounds for arresting Hein, and I certainly will stand witness against him. Will somebody lend me a blanket?"

"Use my outfit," Durham granted, pleased with his victory. "I'm too worked up to sleep. I'll stand watch till morning. It ain't far away. The rest of you turn in."

Durham was so mellowed that he helped Dalke remove his boots and spread out a ground cloth. When daylight came, he was the only one awake. He loafed around for a while and, feeling secure with the coming of day, allowed himself a catnap. But he didn't snooze long. Arousing, he ranged along the creek looking for dry firewood, using it to start a fire. The sleepers did not awake, though he made no effort to be quiet.

Swigging hot coffee aroused his appetite. He went about, nudging the men awake with the toe of his boot, reapplying it with vigor when the initial thrust did not penetrate the spell of Orpheus.

Durham did not awaken Dalke, whose appearance evoked comment by the curious men.

"His face looks like pounded beefsteak."

"That guy ain't fit to go anywhere. He ought to lay up here and rest."

A man laughed. "Yeah, for a week."

"That Dutchman must be as mean as a locoed bull."

"Used his horns on Dalke, looks like."

Laughter.

"Hein didn't like it when we showed up there. I seen that."

"Say, you reckon it might have been Willows who shot at us?"

"Bosh! Why would Willows hang around out here?"

"Bosh yourself. He was headed this way."

"Are you yahoos gonna stand around all mornin' gabbin' like old women?" Durham yelled at them. "Meeker, you're supposed to be the hash-slinger in this outfit. That's why I brought you along. Get at it. I'm as empty as a busted beer barrel."

The plumpest man among them did not jump to obey. He moved at a lesiurely pace down to the creek to wash. Exasperated, Durham watched him, but, having failed on other occasions, knew the futility of trying to hurry him. He also knew that Meeker would remain unruffled by anything that might be said. Words slid off him like grease from a hot pan.

When they had disposed of Meeker's sliced side

meat and pan bread, washed down by copious draughts of coffee, Durham awakened Dalke and asked what he wanted to eat, if anything.

"Whatever you've got," Dalke answered. "I'm hungry."

The cook spent another twenty minutes preparing a special batch, for which Dalke thanked him so civilly that Meeker was surprised. No one else had said anything, though everything he cooked had speedily disappeared. Meanwhile, Dalke had ironed the sore muscles of arms and legs with the heels of his hands, fingered himself testing for injuries, and walked painfully to the creek to wash. He declined offers of assistance.

"I spent the rest of the night thinkin'," Durham informed while Dalke was eating, the other men sitting around. "The boys figure you ain't in shape to do anything but stay here and rest. I got it figured out how we're gonna root out Hein."

"You stay here like he says, Mr. Dalke," one of the men urged. "It's our business to go with Sid, not yours. You'll be as safe here as a preacher in a church."

"Where you men go, I go," Dalke declared firmly. "I feel much better. I'm the one Hein worked over. Besides, that, he laid hands on my wife."

That statement knocked the duck off the rock. Having said too much, Dalke realized belatedly, he had to tell more. But he had recovered sufficiently not to mention Willows and his means of deliverance from Fritz Hein. He felt reluctant to mention Willows at all. Beyond question the man had saved his life.

Tillie Haworth was pleased with herself. She had no intention whatsoever of undertaking a journey on the back of a horse through what she considered to be a vast wilderness. Tillie had made up her mind that when and if she got back to civilization, nothing would ever lure her away from town again. She needed to be among people. Even bums and drifters were more comfortable to be around than Frizt Hein.

Tillie wasn't poor. She had a nest egg stashed away, and she owned a small mortgage on a building occupied by a millinery store and a barbershop. Dean Dalke had recommended her to Fritz Hein. Sniffing at Hein's lure, she had thought she smelled money. Oh, the money was there, but Tillie, who was not a feather-brain, discovered alarming aspects of the situation of which her sniffer had been unaware.

She was convinced that Hein kept his local treasury in the double-locked room. The cellar room had first engaged her attention, but the key ring above the door changed her mind. The "loot" was locked

inside the off-center room. Hard stuff, Tillie surmised, in a generous amount. Enough to make a body
rich. Hein was that kind of gink. He liked to display
affluence. Thinking about it watered the ripe mouth
of the redhead as the thought of food arouses the
hungry.

Yes, she was pleased with herself. She had gotten
rid of Pinkham as slick as bear grease. She knew
the lawmen had another horse, but agreed to the side-
saddle method of departure without over-much fuss,
though somewhat peeved because Pinkham was not
more sympathetic. He didn't want her to make off
with his extra horse. Temporarily, their arrival had
upset her. She feared they would stick around and
spoil her plans. When discovered, she had been sure
she was in for trouble. But the dilemma had been
happily resolved. Indeed, a departure witnessed by
a lawman might prove to be advantageous in the un-
likely event that she ever needed an alibi. Subsequent events at the ranch would not be laid to her.
Her luck was in.

She waited beyond the crest of the knoll until
Pinkham was out of sight, then rode down to the
corral. Her dismounting was not elfin, but Tillie's
equipment was in good working order. She had
noticed that Pinkham's mare was not happy at being
left behind. The animal had remained in the pasture
lane, her head poked over the smaller corral gate.

She looked with favor on the arrival of Tillie and Hein's gelding.

Strategic commander Durham was the first to spot Tillie. He had ordered the posse riders to remain north of the knoll while he reconnoitered. Tillie had just opened the gate to let the willing mare into the corral. The mare accepted Tillie's overtures, allowed herself to be patted, and moseyed on into the larger corral to touch noses with the gelding over the fence.

Durham watched the woman, eyed the house and scanned the premises, thinking himself a cautious and keen-eyed spy. He saw Tillie roll the surrey out of the barn and go back to put a halter on the mare. She led both animals into the barn. The redhead was gone from view for so long that he grew restless and beckoned to the waiting men to come up and join him. Even Dalke dismounted and came up with them. Flattened in the grass, they watched Tillie lead out the harnessed horses and hitch them to the surrey. Durham surmised that the delay had been caused by her unfamiliarity with harness.

"That looks like the marshal's pack animal," Dalke said. "I suppose it isn't, but it looks familiar."

"The floozie is clearing out. Probably Hein gave her the gate."

"Tillie is no floozie. I recommended her to Hein when he came to me looking for help. Tillie is a good cook."

"Good for other things, too." Durham leered. "What's she doin'— loadin' in an axe? What does the dame want with an axe?"

"And a crowbar," one of the men added. "There's already some stuff in that carriage. Looks like baggage."

Tillie led the team to the rear of the house and tied the gelding to a hitching post.

"Holy cow!" Durham exclaimed. "She is gonna chop down the back door! Hein ain't at home. Come on!"

He ran down to his horse. Dalke did not hurry, could not, in fact. They waited impatiently for him to mount.

"What's the rush?" he asked irritably. "Our business is not with Tillie Haworth."

"Mine is." Durham bristled. "I'm gonna find out why that dame is bustin' into Hein's property."

When they rode down from the knoll, the kitchen door stood open. Tillie Haworth was not in sight. At a signal by Durham, the horsemen slowed to a walk, dismounting near the house.

"You come with me," Durham said to Dalke. "The rest of you spread out around the house. If she tries to run, nab her."

Tillie was not in the kitchen. An outbreak of noise farther on identified her whereabouts. Humoring Durham, Dalke walked quietly behind him. Unaware that she was about to have company, engrossed in her assault upon the arsenal door, Tillie was using the crowbar to pry off the metal padlock hasps. As the two men entered the center room, the hasps broke free.

"Howdy, Miss Tillie," the deputy said in a loud voice.

Tillie's heart tried to jump out of her breast, which would have been quite a jump. If it hadn't been in good order, she might have gone to her ancestors then and there. She didn't yell. She squeaked. The crowbar fell across the toes of her right foot. Then she yelled, and the shock may have kept her from fainting.

Durham yanked her away from in front of the door to make room for himself. She staggered back and sank to the floor, grabbing the injured foot with both hands. Her bloom had departed to the interior.

"My foot," she moaned. "Oh, my foot!"

Dalke stepped around her as Durham lifted a booted foot to kick open the arsenal door.

The house blew apart, or seemed to.

The twin blasts of the double-barreled shotgun were terrific. If Dean Dalke knew what killed him, the irrevocable knowledge announced itself in an instant's glimpse of doom. Durham was closer to the shotgun. His kick had turned him sidewise;

his right arm was raised. The shot roared through the gap below his uplifted arm, ripped off a hunk of flesh, muscle and surface bone, and went on to tear a great bloody hole in Dalke's chest. Dalke tumbled back upon the huddled Tillie.

Dazed, hardly aware of what had happened to him, Durham collapsed against the door frame, pawing feebly at the tatters of his bloody shirt. He was only dimly aware of Tillie's screams as she thrust away Dalke's body and scrambled to her feet. She turned to run. But in the hallway she met a wall of incoming men.

Excitement dwindled, as excitement always does. In Hein's house it was pushed away by horror. They were subdued men, those would-be fighters. They did their best amid unfamiliar circumstances, and there was not a man among them who did not hate Fritz Hein when they examined the devilish device he had rigged to guard his arsenal room. A nail had been implanted halfway up the hinge side of the door. From it a cord angled across and around a low cabinet which had been moved out from the wall, thence to the triggers of the gun, around which it had been firmly noosed. The door could be safely opened from within to sufficient width to permit egress, but when the door swung farther, the edge caught and tightened the cord. The shotgun barrels lay flat upon a table, the stock extended. The gun was held firmly by a leaky gunny bag of creek sand.

Deputy Durham was sick, sick, sick. They wrapped him round and round with strips of sheeting. Blood colored the great bandage red. His shock diminishing, he began to hurt.

Durham cursed the day he had come to that murder hole. He accused Tillie Haworth of murder. He vowed to string Fritz Hein to a tree limb and leave him for buzzard meat. He promised to send Tillie to the pen. He cringed from the terrible suspicion in his mind that he had been partly instrumental in causing Dean Dalke's death, refusing to accept the verdict. No, it was Tillie Haworth's fault, and that of murderous Fritz Hein.

Without leadership, the possemen had to decide what to do. They had to get Durham to a doctor. Everyone agreed on that. They found a safe in the arsenal room which looked impregnable without the proper means to open the heavy door. Though curious about the contents, at the moment no one there cared whether Hein lost everything he had, so they gave no thought to leaving men to guard the premises. They also found the pack left in the barn, confirming Dalke's judgment that the mare belonged to the lawmen. This indicated to them that the lawmen would return to the ranch. They exacted information from the distraught Tillie which convinced them that Pinkham and Enright were "after" Hein.

Though encouraging, this information provided no assurance that the rancher would not come back to the ranch. They hated him, but no one wanted to face him without the strength of numbers. Dalke's death and the manner of his dying had been damaging to their nerves. Not a man in the outfit was willing to remain at the ranch. Yet the belief was expressed that the marshals should be informed.

"The Dutchman could come down here with his outfit and wipe us out. That's what he went after, you can bet on that. I wouldn't want to be in them marshals' boots. Why, if a couple of us stuck around here, with all you fellers gone, we might never get away alive. I tell you it ain't worth the risk."

The argument prevailed. They took Sid Durham away. Tillie Haworth went along. They never told her what else was in the arsenal room. She was no longer thinking about getting rich. Dean Dalke had been an important man. No telling what that mean deputy would say about her when they got to town. He had no sympathy at all. There she was, riding in the rear seat of the surrey alongside a roped-in corpse covered with a blanket. Sid Durham sat drooped beside the driver, also roped in to prevent him from falling out, a pillow back of his head, made as comfortable as possible by the solicitous men. Crazy, that was what he was. Why didn't he stop talking and save his strength? She wished he would shut up and die. Her world was in a mess.

It was such a long way to town. Now she dreaded getting there.

Oh God! For nights to come, would she wake up screaming?

14

Enright handed the glasses to Pinkham. "Take a look. Two men moving around outside the tent. I don't see Hein."

Pinkham studied the campsite at length, commenting as he looked.

"There is a cabin back in the woods. He may be there. That's the same kind of set-up they had when I worked for Hein. That tall gink looks like the same hash slinger. A fellow named Hansson or Jansson. Spelled it with two esses. The men called him Swede. . . . Two horses. Both saddled."

"Be nice to ride in through the trees without being looked at over a gunsight."

"An ounce of prevention saves an ounce of lead in the liver, though I don't know of any reason why they should be afraid of us. Do you?"

"Only on account of us being so mean. Lots of people are leery of strangers, particularly when strangers wear badges. We found out what happened to the woman. Why don't we go home?"

"While you're whying, why me this: Why didn't Hein do something about the redhead? Why did he leave a horse in the corral? Why did he take along a pack horse if he was coming to his cow camp? I see two supply wagons up there. Why didn't he even look back when we were trailing him? Seems to me if I had gigged a couple of hombres like Dalke and Sid Durham, I'd look back at least once. Did you see him look back even one time?"

"Moses in the bulrushes, that's enough questions to keep a hen party goin' for half a day. He could have looked back when he was where we couldn't see him."

"That's controlled looking back. You don't do it except when you suspect you're being followed and don't want the trailer to know you know."

Enright groaned. "You make my head bone-tired with your knows. Why didn't I stay home and talk with my cows?"

"Yep, that's Swede! He is acting like a man who thinks someone is coming. Keeps looking off this way. I know how to get to that cabin through the woods. What say I sneak in and have a look-see?"

"Suits me. Scream if you get bit by the Dutchman. I'll run in with a bottle of snake medicine."

A quarter of an hour later, Pinkham was moving quietly down a woodsy slope toward a cabin as large as an Indian long house, a sturdy building constructed of squared logs, shake-roofed and weather-stripped. At one end a stone chimney lifted high above the roof to provide a good draft.

Pinkham almost walked into trouble. He halted abruptly, freezing in his tracks, startled by the sight of a man stalking along outside the near end of the cabin. He was carrying a rifle, and had the manner of a man on the hunt. Before Pinkham recovered from his surprise, the man had gone out of sight toward the camp.

Pinkham had not brought his rifle. He drew his pistol, standing in the partial shelter of a tree trunk as he shouted, "hold on there, Hein! I want to talk—"

The hidden man's reaction added another surprise before Pinkham had fully recovered from the first. He didn't know whether he had forestalled an ambush or merely triggered the gunfire by shouting at the sneaker who had believed himself to be alone. Pinkham had never before heard anyone shoot so fast with a rifle. He withdrew hastily back of the tree, escaping being hit by the margin of a breath.

"Knock it off, you crazy meathead!" he yelled, both frightened and angry. "I'm U.S. Marshal Pinkham. I came here to talk, not to fight."

Down at the camp, someone had shouted. The rifleman stopped shooting, but did not show. Pinkham started to fade back upgrade, trying to shelter himself from the spot where the rifleman had poured lead at him. He was worrying about Enright, afraid that the sounds of battle would draw him into trouble. Perhaps Joe had been right. They should have gone home and left Hein to run his own world as he pleased.

"Listen to me, Hein! I come in peace. We know you didn't kill your wife. We aren't here to bother you. Step out where I can see you. I only want to talk. I don't have a warrant for your arrest."

Lead came within inches of boring through his brain. He thought he actually felt the breeze. The rifleman had changed position. He was moving in for the kill.

The nonplused Pinkham was eating dirt. He was afraid to move, yet had to move or wind up being shot like a huddled rabbit. The sounds of the stalker's movements did not penetrate the silence. Perhaps, as Haworth had implied, Hein had indeed gone out of his mind. In Joe Enright's opinion, rancher Fritz Hein "had blown his lid."

Over what? Had Lotus provided the spark for a smoldering fuse?

He moved suddenly to his left, darting for another tree, then ran ingloriously from the cabin area, regardless of noise, charging away like a stampeding steer. Behind him the woods came alive with rifle noises. They remained fixed. The shooter did not pursue him. Nor was there any further shouting.

Pinkham circled in the timber, trying to return to

the place where he had parted with Enright. He
missed on the first try and had to hunt, being quiet
about it, hesitating to call out. Enright was not a
tenderfoot. He would not fire at a sound.

The silence of the woods became disturbing. Yet
when it gave way to an outbreak of firing nearer the
camp, Pinkham's nerves jumped in apprehension.
Joe? Or someone shooting at Joe?

The suspense intensified when he found his horse
tied to a sapling. Enright was not there. Neither
was Enright's horse.

Pinkham yanked his rifle from the boot and loped
toward the campsite along the scraggly rim of timber. He hadn't gone far before he came upon Enright's horse standing away from the woods, reins
trailing. The gelding was nervous. After a turn of
the head which identified Pinkham, the horse looked
again toward the campsite, ears pricked forward.
At that moment shouting erupted. Pinkham thought
he heard Enright. He put on speed. Ahead, a running man broke from the timber. The move triggered
a rifle shot, the sound oddly flattened by the trees.
The running man seemed to stumble, then went
ahead a half-dozen faltering strides before he fell.

Joe Enright!

Pinkham could not go out to him, did not know
whether he was alive or dead. He was down out
of sight. The grassland offered no sign.

A great sob welled up in Pinkham's throat. Raging, he went into the trees; went not in a heedless charge, but as the ferret goes, moving toward the spot where he thought the rifleman had fired. The woods were deceptive. For a while he heard nothing but the sounds of his own making, saw nothing but trees and brush. Then in swift succession voices broke into shouting, and a shot ripped out, succeeded by a choking, nerve-chewing silence. He crept on, his rifle ready, straining at the disturbing quiet.

Surprisingly near, a man let out a roaring curse. Pinkham dropped to the ground. A low branch raked his face.

The same voice lifted in a angry wail. "Bert! Who has done this awful thing?"

"Swede, is that you in there? *Jansson?*"

The silence of suspicion, perhaps of fear.

"Hold your fire, Jansson. Is someone hurt?"

Jansson swore. "Hurt? You killed Bert Parker. He is deader than a rock."

"Not me, Swede. I never fired a shot."

"Den the other one did it. Me and Bert saw two of you. Why you tried to murder us?"

"It's the other way around, Swede. We didn't shoot at you. You shot at us. My partner was hit. He fell out there in the grass. He may be dead or dying while we squat here and yell at each other. Swede, I'm coming in."

"No you ain't. Who the hell are you?"

"Suds Pinkham. I used to work for Hein. You should remember me. I'm a U.S. marshal. My partner is a deputy. We didn't come here to shoot. We came to talk to Hein."

"Hein ain't here. He left half an hour ago."

"No need to cover for him, Swede. I know about Hein."

"What you mean, cover? He left with a pack horse before Bert got back. Bert saw you fellers comin'. We wait. You don't come. All at once, bang-bang in the woods. Nobody here but me and Bert. You come to murder us. You're a liar, Pinkham. You don't fool me."

"Listen, knothead! I haven't fired a shot."

"Someone hollerin' out in the grass. 'Tain't me."

Pinkham listened. "It's Joe!" he shouted in a great surge of relief. "He is alive. I'm going out there, Swede. Stay where you are if you don't trust me, but hold your fire."

He moved with care, unsure of Jansson, puzzled by Hein's silence, wondering if the rancher were waiting for him to show or whether he had departed in the same mysterious manner he had come. Certainly he had not showed himself to Jansson. Who had killed Bert Parker? Not Joe Enright, unless he had fired in self-defense. Enright had done no shooting after he had been hit.

Pinkham ran out to the tent, went around it to the chuck wagon and paused there, protected from attack on the woods side. He cupped his hands around his mouth. "Joe, where are you?"

"Is that you, Pink?"

The faint reply came from off in the grassland east of the woods, but Enright did not reveal himself. "You all right, Pink?"

Dang his hide! Thinking about me instead of himself.

"Are you hurt bad?"

"Somebody went out of there, Pink. A horse came out of the woods farther north. Headed out at a run."

Pinkham let out a deep breath. He yelled toward Jansson. "Swede, we're all right now. You can come out. I'm going to take care of my pard."

As he spoke, a hatless head lifted into sight above the grass. Enright had been hidden in what seemed to be a small swale. Pinkham ran.

"What was all that fuss?" Enright wanted to know. He tried to stand. Pinkham reached for him, seeing blood on his left side. Enright could not stay on his feet.

"Hey, I can't walk! I was afraid of that. Stepped into a hole. Twisted my leg when I fell."

"Hold still, dang it! Let me look at your side."

Pinkham was pulling at the bloody shirt. "Why do you have to wear a vest in this hot weather?"

"Stop tryin' to undress me. It's my leg that hurts. Go cut a forked stick so I can walk."

"You're bleeding."

"Good blood. Look how red it is. It's only a slice. I know that without lookin'. Hey, there's that beanpole comin' out of the trees. Go get him. I can use him for a cane."

Pinkham stood up and looked. "That's Swede Jansson. He is mad at us. He thinks we killed his sidekick, fellow named Bert Parker. I know Swede. I didn't know Parker."

"Moses on the mountain! Somebody got killed? You must have done it, Pink. I didn't shoot."

"Neither did I. Unless Jansson killed him by mistake, it was Fritz Hein. I surprised him in the woods, and he tried to kill me."

"What? I couldn't tell who the rider was. I was afraid to rear up for a good look. You mean he shot one of his own men?"

"I told you he was playing games. Parker must have seen him, and he didn't want to be seen. I can't read his nutty mind, but he sure tried to kill me when I yelled at him. He was sneaking around the cabin in the woods. Neither of those men at the camp knew he was there. That cut should be bandaged, Joe. You're losing a lot of blood."

"Ah, it's already sealin' over. I didn't bring along a bed sheet. Have you got an extra? Hey, that Swede gink is edgin' out this way, head stuck out like a turkey. Got his big gun, too. Maybe he intends to make us dance a bullet jig."

"Come on, Swede," Pinkham called. "We're harmless. My partner got creased, and he hurt his leg."

Jansson came nearer, a determined man approaching the uncertain. They watched him, waiting. When he was near enough to speak without shouting, Pinkham said, "Relax, man, or make up your mind to use your gun. I'm not going to spend the rest of the day arguing with you. Which one of you shot my pard?"

Jansson's pale blue eyes were hostile. "I never. I wish I did. He killed Bert Parker."

"Not me, Swedey," Enright denied. "Come over here, and I'll let you smell my pistol, and when you do I'll pull the trigger. My rifle is still in the saddle boot. That was rifle fire in there, not six-gun stuff."

The hostile gaze turned to Pinkham.

"I told you already, Swede. I don't intend to tell you again. If you want me to, I'll help carry Parker down to the tent."

Jansson's brow corrugated. "Fonny kind of law marshal. Come in here to shoot us. We done nothing."

Enright's hand came up from his side as he sat on the ground. It held a pistol. "Put down your rifle, you stubborn buzzard. *Put it down!*"

Jansson stepped back a pace, looking as though he had been clubbed.

Pinkham went toward him. "Do as he says, Swede.

We're tired of fooling around. I think Hein went to bring the rest of the crew."

"Hein?" gasped the bewildered Jansson. "You talk like you got no sense at all."

He threw down the rifle, stubborn and angry. Pinkham picked it up. Enright put away his pistol.

"Go get my horse, Pink. If you help me into the saddle, I can make it out of here. I reckon we don't have much time. How far off are your men, Mr. Jansson?"

Jansson shook his head as if to rattle his brains loose. "The boss didn't go after no men. He wasn't here. I told Pinkham he left half an hour ago."

"That doesn't mean he never came back," Enright said as Pinkham started off to bring the horses.

"Not so. I would have seen his horse."

"He probably rode a broomstick. Why don't you start acting like a human being and get me something to wrap myself with? A clean undershirt will do, if you ever wear anything clean. Be extravagent. Rip a blanket into strips. Go on, man. I'll pay for the stuff."

"For why should I help you? You kill—"

"All right, forget it. How far is it to where your crew are working?"

"I don't know. They're around everywhere."

"How many?"

"Ten besides me and Bert."

"Maybe I ought to shoot you now and reduce

the odds. Your boss has turned outlaw, Jansson. What do you reckon he will tell the crew? That two lawmen shot your pard? That's what you believe."

Jansson wall-eyed him. "You think I'm a dumbhead?"

"I think you're acting like one. Pink is coming with our broncs. Try to get it through your head that he saw Hein in the woods, and I saw Hein cut out of the woods farther north and ride off like a horse thief being chased by a posse. For some reason, Hein shot your sidekick. You may be next. If I was in your boots, I'd climb on one of them saddled horses and head for Chicago. If you stay here, don't forget to look behind you. And stay out of the woods."

Not knowing what to believe, Jansson stood back watching while Pinkham assisted Enright into the saddle. He did not offer to help.

"Does this rifle belong to you?" Pinkham inquired.

Jansson shook his head.

"Then we'll take it along to use on Hein if he decides to chase us. Don't you come, Swede. Good cooks are scarce."

"Remember what I said," Enright called back as they rode away. "Grab your war bag and take a ship back to Sweden. Your boss had gone loco."

"I suppose we ought to find a place in the timber where we can hole up for a while," Pinkham said.

"You're in no shape to travel. I doubt that Hein would try to track us through the woods, but we'd better not take any chances. Swede is headed back to camp. I'll bet you he is talking to himself."

"I'd talk to myself if I was beginning to believe the gink I worked for had squirrels in his head. I wonder why Hein shot one of his own men. Maybe he *has* gone crazy."

"Mistake, probably. Thought it was me."

Meanwhile, the bufuddled cook had returned to the camp. He went into the woods to carry out Parker's body and place it in the shade of the tent. He removed the gunbelt, and was wondering whether to take off Parker's boots. His head hurt. Perplexed by the strange happenings and grieved by Parker's death, as he stood pondering he glanced out through the open end of the tent at the north and was further disturbed by the sight of a band of horsemen roaring toward the camp. Not an unfamiliar sight, but on this occasion he felt strangely panicky. He did not want to face Fritz Hein. Snatching up Parker's gunbelt, he ran into the woods.

The incoming crew immediately discovered the body in the tent. Alarmed, enraged and puzzled, they searched the near woods, fearful of finding Jansson's corpse. Fritz Hein was not with them.

There was no order to the search until Gabe Kinney shouted them out into the open. A grizzled, hard-bitten, stocky type, the foreman looked about

fifty but was only thirty-six. Though as puzzled as
the rest, he was top dog and everyone knew it.
He was accustomed to handling men. Unable to
answer their questions, he cooled their excitement,
stating in plain language that he didn't know any
more about the situation than they, refused to specu-
late openly and led them forth along the benchland
where grass and timber grudgingly joined. There
he posted them in pairs, with the two armed men
left at the cow camp. He stationed them in places
of advantage which afforded a long view of the
immediate area, with orders to rally at a focal point
if alerted by two pistol shots. He rode on alone as
far as The Devil's Finger. With the help of a small
pocket 'scope, he saw hills, rolling grassland, cattle
by the hundreds, but no departing raiders.

It hadn't been a true raid. He knew that much.
The camp was in order. A quick visual survey had
convinced him nothing had been taken.

He wondered what to do about Parker's body.
Take it down to the ranch for burial? Yeah, they
ought to do that. Let Hein decide about the rest.
Kinney made a forceful remark as the realization
struck him—they were without a cook! There was not
another man in the crew capable of accomplishing
anything more than internal ruin.

He had ridden only a short distance on his return
trip when he saw the whole outfit hightailing toward
him—even the two men left at the camp.

He spurred to meet them.

"Hey!" someone yelled when they were close enough to holler. "Old Swede has quit the job. He says he ain't gonna work no more for Hein. We've lost our hash slinger."

Kinney swore. At the moment he was sure that Jansson had killed Bert Parker.

15

A voice called from the timber near the cow camp tent.

"Don't shoot, fallers! It's me, Thor Jansson."

Two startled cowhands looked and saw nothing but trees and brush.

"Swede? Dang your ornery hide, come out of there!"

Jansson came forth in the manner of a man walking barefoot on hot coals. He stopped just outside the timber cover to inquire nervously, "Where is the boss?"

"At the ranch, I reckon. Why you ask a fool thing like that?"

Jansson looked perplexed. "Didn't he come back with you?"

"You must be drunk! What happened to Bert?"

Jansson came nearer. He was looking everywhere except at them, as if expecting Fritz Hein to pop forth. "He got shot."

"We know that, dumbhead. Who shot him? Where

you been—hiding out in them woods? Did you kill Bert?"

"I quit," Jansson announced stolidly. "Bert was my friend. I do not hurt him. I taken him away and bury him like Christian."

"Quit! What's the matter with you, dumbhead? You act like you're scared of your shadder. Did you and Bert get into a fuss? Kinney and the boys are out lookin' for you. You have made a heap of trouble."

"No fuss. You call me dumbhead once more, I make you know who is dumbhead. I take Bert. He was my friend. You not my friends. Get out of my way or I break your heads. I take Bert."

They stepped aside as he advanced determinedly. His eyes were bloodshot and angry, his features grimly set.

"Take him where? Kinney ain't here, Swede. You got no right— Hey, stay away from them horses! Who says you can quit? Who is gonna cook our meals?"

"What you quittin' for? What was you doin' in them woods?"

"Marshals," Jansson mumbled. "Them men was United States marshals."

He was letting down a rope in order to lead out the saddled horses.

The puzzled cowhands stared at each other, then at him. "You tellin' us a bunch of marshals raided our cow camp?" demanded the more talkative one.

"No raid. Big fight in the woods. Bert got killed. They let me go. One of them was shot. Blood all over his shirt."

"Goshamighty! You mean they jumped Bert and he shot one of 'em? What's he done? Why was they after him?"

"They swore they never shot him. I quit. I want no more of this job. I get job some place else. I good cook. I get job."

Without waiting or asking for assistance that was not volunteered, Jansson had lifted Parker's body and draped it across a saddle. He started to secure the dangling hands and legs. The horse rolled its eyes and looked around, but did not move away.

"You oughtn't do that. Kinney will get onto us if you take Bert away."

The protest was without force. Jansson paid no attention except to assert, "Kinney ain't my boss no more. Hein ain't my boss. Bert don't have no boss. I take care of him."

"Marshals— Say, Kinney ought to know about this. I reckon we ought to go tell him. What was they really after, Swede?"

"Mebby you," the cook answered contrarily. "I get my belongings out of wagon now. I take only what belongs to me and Bert. You don't have to watch. I am not a thief."

"Aw, come on, Swede; we never said—"

"Go tell Kinney marshals went into the woods. He won't find them out there."

He made a sweeping gesture indicating a lot of grassland. "You tell him what I say. You jump the marshals, you all in bad fix. They say they don't shoot Bert. I think mebby they right. Something bad happen here. I quit. You go tell Kinney."

The cowhands looked at each other, nodded and topped their horses, riding off without saying so long or once looking back.

"Danged funny," the more talkative one said to his partner. "Swede is all worked up. Wonder why them marshals was gunnin' for Bert."

"Swede said they wasn't."

"Well, it wasn't no porkypine that shot him. Do you know where Bert came from? He must have got into trouble 'fore he came here. Seemed like a nice feller."

His partner didn't know much, but was willing to guess.

"He was into somethin' back yonder, you can bet on that. Marshals don't ride around shootin' folks 'less they got a reason. Comin' way up here! Man, that's a job of trackin'. I bet they been after him a long time. You just never know about a man. The feller you bunk next to may be a killer or a thief, mebby both."

Whereupon they fell silent, realizing that neither knew overly much about the other.

16

Joe Enright's seat was on the hard rock of a shelf-like ledge, his back against a cliff. He was bare to the waist, the red furrow along his ribs open to the air. Besides him lay his folded undershirt, bloody from use in dabbing away droolings from the wound. It had started to seal and would have stopped bleeding if the edges had been pulled together. Lacking stitches, it would be slow to heal and leave a wide scar.

It was a painful wound, but not dangerous unless it became infected. If he had had two good legs, Enright would have padded the slice with the undershirt, wrapped his body with something to hold the pad in place, possibly Pinkham's undershirt, and headed out of there rather than risk a clash with Fritz Hein.

Enright didn't know what to do about the leg. Injured ligaments were giving him Hail Columbia, but wouldn't hurt worse in the saddle than out of it, provided they were not under any strain. He needed to shed his boot. It was too full of foot.

He wriggled about, trying to find a formation on the ledge that would serve as a bootjack. Nothing worked. He would have to wait for Pinkham or cut off the boot top, which he hoped to avoid. Trying to bend the leg so he could reach the boot with his hands made him yowl. Grumbling aloud, he tried to think of some way out of his predicament.

Pinkham had been gone for nearly two hours. Enright worried, talking to himself about stumble-bums who fell over their own feet. He wished he had never heard of Fritz Hein.

He sat between two rifles, his own and the one taken from Thor Jansson. His back was well protected, and he had a good view of the approach to the ledge. Their horses were concealed in timber off at the right. Pinkham had gone back toward the cow camp on foot.

"Estimating what Hein will do is like trying to control the wind. I'm not going to hole up and wait for him to find us. I'm going to meet him when he isn't ready."

Enright thought Pinkham made good sense but was grumpy because he couldn't go along. "For all the good I've done, you would be better off if you had left me at home."

He had thought himself into a foul humor by the time his bloodshot orbs detected movement in the brush of a small gully below the ledge. His rifle was trained on the spot when Pinkham came into view. Pink approached at a jogging run. He started to shout before he came up beneath the ledge.

"I'm going after my horse. There is nobody at the cow camp."

"Hold on a ding-dang minute!" Enright roared. "You ain't goin' out there and leave me roostin' on this ding-dang rock!"

Pinkham was already past the ledge. "Never said I was. I'll fetch your crowbait. You can follow slow."

"Go suck a goose egg!" Enright yelled after him. "If you get me into the saddle, I can ride as fast as you can."

Realizing that he had reared up on his feet, he hobbled to the edge of his rocky roost and angrily hooked a boot heel over the rim, yanking, mightily, evoking a yowl of pain. Much to his surprise, the swollen foot came free and the boot tumbled down from the ledge. Balancing precariously on the socked foot, his face screwed up more than that of a hired wailer at a funeral, by the same method he loosened the other boot, managing to catch it before it joined its fellow below the ledge.

Loosening, his belt, he dropped his levis without further aggravating the hurt leg. He was sitting as naked as a molting rooster from the waist down, undertaking to wrap the injured member with his drawers, when he heard Pinkham returning with the horses.

"Why did you throw away your boot?" Pinkham called.

"I didn't. It went down to look for Fritz Hein. Stop askin' fool questions and come help me wrap this confounded leg."

Pinkham climbed. "Wrap it with what?"

"An old woman's drawers, if you brought an old woman. If you didn't, take off your pants and give me yours."

"I wear short ones in the summer. They only come to my knees."

"I don't care where they come to. Shuck 'em. Peel off your undershirt while you're at it. I've figured a way to hold my ribs together."

"Think I'm gonna strip in front of you? You're an innocent child, not used to looking at naked men."

"Then I won't be any less innocent after beholdin' you."

Pinkham was shedding his clothes. "That's not the neatest bandage I ever saw. What are the buttons for?"

"For your lip. Why do you keep talkin' around the mulberry bush? What went haywire?"

"I figured wrong. Nobody tried to track us. The camp is deserted. We ran from nothing."

"Then it is time to back-track."

"Seems so. Anyway, you got some time to rest."

"Oh, sure, use me for an excuse. You ought to know I dont' expect you to be right more than half the time."

"I scouted the woods around the camp. No dead man. The horses are gone from that rope pen."

"Blast it, lay hold of this pad! I can't keep the blankety-blank thing in place while I wind on my shirt. . . . There, that ought to do it. Tie the sleeves in a knot. . . . You can put on your pants now. I'm through lookin'. What do you think they're up to?"

"My waist. That's as high as pants go. You can't take 'em off over your head. How do you expect to get yours back on over all that bolt goods?"

"Slit the leg at the seam. Hang onto one leg while I do the cutting."

"Hein sure knew we were tailing him."

"That's hard to figure out, with my leg remindin' me every minute. Kinda looks like the redhead had him pegged. Going after Willows. Doesn't want company. Must have thought he was plugging you when he shot his own man."

"Your horse is gonna climb the sky when he sees you. You look like something that ought to be buried. What do I do—carry you down the ledge piggyback?"

"You hang onto my shirttail knot so I won't fall. I want to live long enough to get back on grass, where Hein's outfit can see to shoot me in the head instead of slicing meat off my ribs."

"I'm not afraid of a shooter I can see."

"Well, I am, if Hein's outfit has any more knot-heads like Jansson. Funny he left the camp. You say the body was gone?"

"I said I didn't find it. The two horses were gone."

"Crawlin' crawdads, this wrapping helps my leg! I may be a good man again in a couple of years if I can get rid of you. Ow-itch!"

"Don't put all your weight on it! Hobble, dang it."

They descended without great difficulty, Pinkham going first, supporting Enright from below. When they reached the horses, he got down on all fours so Enright could step on his back with the good leg, hang onto the saddle horn and swing the bandaged leg over the horse's rump. At the last minute they remembered to retrieve Enright's boot.

The cow camp was still deserted when they reached the grassland.

"Hein or no Hein, we've got to take time to eat," Pinkham said. "I'm empty as a hollow beer barrel, and I know you are, too. When I worked for this outfit, they used to keep fresh meat in a box where the spring gushes out of the mountain. I'll lift you off so you can rest while I knock together some grub. How you feeling?"

"I've felt better, but not often. I reckon you're thinking that Hein is long gone. He foxed us good."

"At the cost of a man."

Enright was sitting on the ground eating steak and gravy when he called attention to a band of horsemen approaching from the south. Apparently they had been riding leisurely until they sighted the two horses at the camp.

"Good-sized bunch," he commented. "It has to be Hein's crew. I'll bid you goodbye while I have some time left."

Pinkham kept on eating. "Nice to die with a full stomach."

"Those cowpokes are pounding leather. Hope they don't start shooting before they come in to look us over."

"Fellow named Gabe Kenney's riding in front. He was the foreman when I worked for Hein. I may know some more of them."

"Just like we figured, Hein isn't with them. Maybe that will help."

The riders did not slow down as they neared the camp. They came up in a flurry, hauling in with much bustle but no show of arms, though their manners was not compounded of sweetness and light. Unfriendly eyes examined Enright's bandage and leg wrappings. The latter had been considerably improved by strips torn from a blanket taken from the supply wagon.

"Howdy, Kinney," Pinkham greeted him. "We helped ourselves to grub. Hadn't eaten since last night. Getting kind of empty."

"Suds Pinkham!" offered a lantern-jawed rider. "You've growed up some since I seen you last."

"How are you, Pruitt? This is my partner, Joe Enright. He got creased by lead and fell into a gopher hole."

They were out of their saddles, crowding forward to the tent, Kinney in the fore. Pinkham had pinned on his badge.

"Marshals!" Pruitt exclaimed incredulously. "Are you the marshals Swede was talkin' about? Well, I'll be a muley horn. How come you shot up our camp?"

"We never fired a shot," Enright said, giving him a cool stare. "Before you start accusin' folks, why don't you drape yourselves around and listen to our fairy tale?"

"One of my boys was killed," Kinney said gruffly.

"Not by us," Pinkham told him. "Parker or Jansson may have tried to kill Enright. Somebody did. I give you my word we didn't burn any powder. Where is boss man Hein?"

"I'm in charge here. I haven't seen the boss for a month. What I want to know is: Why are you men squattin' in our camp?"

"Before he answers, I have something else to say," Enright put in. "I'm wearing a blanket and a clean apron and a shirt Pinkham took out of your supply wagon. I aim to pay for them. A while back we borrowed a rifle from your cook. Pink put it back in the wagon. By the way, where is friend Jansson?"

"According to Smith and Harris, he quit the job. Took away Bert Parker's corpse. You men scared hell out of Swede. What you got on him and Parker?"

"Not a thing. He is not scared of us. He is scared of the woods shooter who got rid of Parker, unless Jansson shot him by mistake. Has Mrs. Hein been staying up here with you? Maybe in the woods cabin?"

"What's it to you?"

"She sent word to Lotus Flower that she was sick and wanted to see her. Maybe she mentioned that to you."

"Maybe she did. That still don't tie up with you."

"Yes, it does. Lotus sent the message to me. My name was also mentioned. Did Mrs. Hein tell you about that?"

"No. She didn't do much talkin'. Never did. She stayed here about a week, then went home. We figured she got sore at the boss. She was feelin' sick, no question about that. Didn't help much with the cookin', which ain't her usual style."

"She didn't go home. She went up on The Devil's Finger. I suppose the climb was too much for her. She died up there. Hein buried her earlier this morning under a pile of rocks."

"Goshamighty!"

The foreman's exclamation topped their oh's and

ah's. They shifted about uneasily, staring at each other and at the lawmen. Questions jumped around like grasshoppers with hot feet. From among them Pinkham selected the one from Kinney.

"Sure Hein was up there. We ought to know. We followed him from the ranch. And he was right here in these woods a while back. I saw him. He blame near emptied a rifle at me. If we want to put it to a vote, I say he shot your man Parker. I believe Jansson thinks so, too. I think that is why he quit."

It was too much. Kinney took off his hat, wiped his brow and puffed out his cheeks.

"What are we into? Why was you followin' the boss?"

"Do you know a man named Willows? Calls himself that."

"I've seen him. He has been to the ranch. I calculate nobody knows him. He don't talk about his-self."

"Did he come to the ranch before Lotus married Dalke?"

"That's when he came. Dunno that he has been there since. I calculate you wouldn't expect me to know what goes on down there when I ain't around?"

"Dalke had a run-in with Willows, maybe on account of Lotus. They had Willows in jail, but he broke out. Evidently he lives out this way. Joe and

I think that's where Hein is going. Does anybody here know where that might be?"

Kinney's skepticism had changed to bewilderment. "Why would the boss go after Willows?"

"I'll explain if you tell me whether Hein ever followed Willows or talked about him to you."

"Yeah, he follered him. Dunno why, except I could see the boss don't like him. Said he'd been up in the high country between the snake's tail and the Elk. I calculate he meant the Little Snake."

"Kinney, Joe and I have got to get out of here. Lotus came out to see Mrs. Hein. Willows grabbed her. I think Hein has gone after him. It's a sticky business. Dean Dalke came ramming into the ranch with a posse. Apparently he and Hein got into a fight, and Hein cut loose on them with a gun. Killed Dalke's horse. Do any of you men know the high country Kinney mentioned?"

"I do," Pruitt answered. "My pappy was a mountain man. Took me huntin' before I could walk."

"Haw!" a listener blared. "What did you do—crawl?"

"Went on all fours," Pruitt declared solemnly. "I could keep up with the best hound dog pappy had. He had lots of 'em."

Pinkham looked at the foreman. "How about it? May Pruitt go with us? That is, if he is willing."

"You askin' us to take sides against the boss?"

"I'm asking you to help find Lotus. Some of you

know her. She is in trouble. Besides, Hein may need help. I think Willows is dangerous."

"Lemme go, Gabe," Pruitt said. "I'm willin'."

"We'll all go. I know something about the country. Smith you and Harris stay here and look after things. Dennis, sack up some grub. We may be gone two or three days. Fetch your bedrolls, and what else you want to take along. Hop to it, yahoos. Pinkham is itchin' to get goin'."

Pinkham was grateful. "Thanks, Kinney. I won't forget this."

"Not doin' it for you," the foreman replied curtly. "I ain't heard the whole fairy tale yet. If it don't turn out like you say, that badge ain't gonna do you no good."

"That's telling him," Enright stated gravely. "Bear down on him. He gets me into more trouble than a bear in a bee tree."

Kinney eyed him dourly, then permitted his weathered face to crack slightly at the corners.

17

By nightfall Fritz Hein was no less than thirty miles from his cow camp on the benchlands. He traveled as long as he could see before stopping for the night. There was no water in the sparsely grassed swale huddled forlornly below a serrated chine, but he had given the animals time to drink at the last small stream crossing and carried plenty for himself. Graze was too poor for a stake-out, so he hobbled the animals to allow wider range and made short shrift of his own needs, following the mechanics of habit rather than the requirements of appetite. His mind was not on the preparation of food or conditions for sleep. He was a man obsessed.

Hein stopped traveling because he could not find his way by night; stopped unwillingly. By mid-morning of the following day he should arrive at a clear mountain spring which was not his goal but the starting place of the real hunt. On a former occasion he had doggedly traced the stream to its source, a time-consuming search which had depleted his strength, bruised his flesh, and left him sullen in the anger of frustration.

He had not found Will of the Willows. Somewhere along the mountain stream he had lost Willows after hours of painstaking trailing.

Though his two attempts to track Willows had not been entirely successful, he knew he had come near the hideaway. Next time out he would find it. But there had been no next time. A confrontation got in the way of that.

When it occurred, Hein had been surprised and enraged. He had expected demands, not accusations and expressions of hate. He had dismissed the fellow Anderson with contempt, handing out the money as a pittance to a whining beggar.

"Show your face here again, I shoodt you. *Heraus!*"

So the low-life had lost the sight in one eye. Hein had not intended to maim him, but felt no regret. He was a nothing, who deserved what he got. Both of them were nothings, birds of a feather. Were they still running together as they had of old? The association had run them into the penitentiary and might well do so again.

Hein did not think of these events as in any way related to his own dealings in the past. He blamed everyone else for interference in his life—Dalke, Pinkham, Enright, Anderson, Willows, even Faith and Lotus Flower. He wasn't afraid of Willows, but sensed he was the most dangerous.

The swine had taken Lotus Flower away. Hein was so sure of himself in that respect that only the presence of Lotus would have convinced him otherwise. The thought of her in Willows' possession drove him berserk. He couldn't bear it. *Ach Gott, he* should have brought a whip. . . .

He lay down to sleep and found it difficult to compose an uneasy mind. The question of his wife's absence had been answered. She was out of his life at last. There was no sadness, no sense of loss. When the crew returned to the ranch, he would make out with Jansson's cooking until he found someone to take Faith's place. He took it for granted that Tillie Haworth had gone off with the posse, or perhaps with Willows in Lotus Flower's buggy. She had money to bribe her way.

By *himmel,* one day she would pay back every cent of the unearned bonus. There would be a day of recompense.

He hadn't bothered about the stocking-legged bay left in the corral. Starface was a gate opener. When he felt the need for pasture grass, he would nose open the hand slide of the swinging gate of the corral and amble into the lane.

Hein was up with the dawn. The Willows fixation urged immediate departure. But he was practical, methodical. And he was hungry. He ate adequately of hard cured ham, bread brought from the ranch, drank heavily sugared coffee, and munched dried prunes as he rode, having stuffed the pocket of his loose canvas jacket with the fruit. As expected, he reached a small tributary of the Little Snake around ten o'clock. An half-hour later he left the pack horse tied to a sapling at a place where he could ride across the stream without endangering the roan's legs. He dismounted, tied the roan, took out his rifle to sling it across his shoulders and untied the bowie knife from the saddle horn. Knife in hand, he moved upstream through the boscage along the bank.

When Hein had set his shotgun trap at the ranch, he did so in full awareness of what would happen to anyone who broke open the arsenal room door. Let the would-be thief beware. If he were killed outright or lay maimed and bleeding out his life on the floor, so be it. A dead thief could steal no more. Breaking and entering would have been punished. Hein had taken pleasure in laying his trap. Honest men were in no danger. It never occurred to him to consider what might happen if he did not return.

Near some willows, in open view, Hein came upon an abandoned buggy beside a small silent waterflow merging gently with the mountain stream, the effluence hidden by the old trees and their offspring.

Excitement was a light streaking through his

brain. He examined the rig, found evidences that it had been packed with supplies, left it to hurry along an animal trail which wound upward alongside the sneaky rivulet which concealed itself at times among the timbered crags.

A thousand feet higher, the searcher approached a narrow, rock-slabbed defile located below an almost perfect U of greenery. The rock slit was no wider than a dozen feet adjacent to the worn-down, debris-strewn narrows which confined the clear waters of the brook. The defile opened into a high, narrow valley slanting upward between stupendous heights, the high-flung ramparts of the abutting mountains. The walls of the hidden valley were green-clad when the steeps permitted, apparently inaccessible save through the narrow defile.

Could human beings survive in such a place through a pitiless winter? The great slit would be piled deep with snow. Yet a mountain fastness difficult to find could be made almost impregnable to attack.

Hein used his glasses, searching for a sentinel. There was none. Willows did not live in fear.

With the help of the glasses, he studied a sample of man's handiwork, a structure planted against a bulging cliff at the north, a slanting room of logs supported by huge log pillars. The shelter was open at one end and at the front. The closed end was part of a continuing structure entirely enclosed.

There were no visible windows, no door. The openings were beneath the log roof of the shelter.

Three horses grazed far up the valley. Near them were six bovines, four full grown, two who appeared to be yearlings. Stolen stock, Hein surmised. Nothing about Willows could be honest.

As he was tracing the brook to the upper limit of the valley, where it was lost to sight, a movement at the edge of his vision caused him to shift the glasses. Lotus Flower had come out from beneath the shelter. She carried a wooden bucket across to the channel of the brook, dipped it full and went back into the building.

The sight of her sent blood racing through his veins. He had found his "liddle Lotus."

Impatience seized him. Caution became an unbearable restraint. He studied the terrain, the abutting slopes and steeps, seeking a way to approach the building in secret. There was no way unless he chose to wait for dark. He would not wait.

He watched through minutes of dragging irritation. Nothing happened. Lotus did not appear again. Inertness mocked him.

He studied the open shelter, a log-roofed shed. Ricked firewood lined the rear. It offered no place for a man to hide.

He studied the enclosed building. The walls were solid, windowless. He was unable to discover any chink or crevice through which eyes could look out at him from inside. The impatient invader convinced himself that Lotus was there alone.

Hein realized that his own position in the defile was risky. If Willows were indeed away temporarily, he would not be gone long, for Lotus had been left free to range. Hein could not believe she was there by her own choice. A prisoner or a prize. *Ach*, Willows was away. No doubt of that. The appaloosa he had ridden on all his trips to the ranch was not one of three horses up the valley. Hein had never seen the grazing black.

A returning Willows would trap him in the valley! *Ach*, so. Let the unwary outlaw ride into his waiting gun. Again he wished he had brought a whip.

Ah, poor lost Lotus. She would be afraid to run off into the terrible hills.

Apparently only the mountains watched the approach of the armed invader. He did not dally. Having made up his mind, he moved decisively. The peace of nature remained undisturbed, a serenity too majestic for disruption by a puny human bent on murder.

The bulging eyes fixed upon the waiting shelter. Lotus Flower remained inside the enclosure. As Hein came near, he thought he heard her moving about inside. She was indeed alone. He gloated over the thought, reveling in the prospect of surprise.

The log structure was not new but old, quite old, weathered by the years.

Now he could see an open door beneath the shelter. He stole toward it, strangely quiet, an animal moving toward his prey. The log structure was now as quiet as the barren rock where Faith Hein had gone to die.

18

Empty! Lotus Flower was not in the log shelter.

Fritz Hein halted inside the doorway, goggling at the logged-in space. The windowless shelter was sparsely furnished with hand-wrought small benches and a table. A thin-jacketed stove was the only bought piece. It was flat on top for cooking, with a Dutch oven.

A candle burned in a bottle holder which stood on a section of log away from the walls in a corner. By its light Hein saw that the rear wall was also made of logs, not the side of a cliff which he had expected to see. Searching eyes examined a door center of the wall. The door was closed.

Hein cautiously put out a foot as if testing the dirt floor for a trap. Intimations of danger made him warier still. He examined the verdict of his senses, yet rebelled against it, hungering for action to end the devastating silence.

A small sound on the other side of the door rooted

him. He pointed the rifle. His head reared back like a rattler recoiling to strike as a flap in the door fell away. His nerves jumped. The rifle muzzle centered on the dark opening.

A voice jumped forth. "Well, Hein, you made it at last."

He restrained the impulse to shoot. Shooting would be futile. The speaker would not stand in line with the opening. Hein hated futility.

"Put your rifle on the table and take off your gunbelt."

He thought of bolting back into the shed. Desperation urged him to do so. Surrender was unthinkable. Mesmerized by the uncanny, he thought the invisible speaker read his mind.

"One step toward the shed and I'll blow off your head. This is a shotgun, Hein. Two barrels. Hammer cocked. I see you good."

Sweat popped out on his brow. His body flushed inside the jacket held loosely across his chest by the top button.

"Coom oudt, Villows! I vant to talk mit you."

"You didn't come to talk. You came after the Chinese gal. Get rid of your guns. I'll cripple you; I won't kill you. Not yet."

Hein side-stepped to the table, his feet reluctant. He didn't chide himself for walking into a trap. He was shouting silent curses at the creature who had trapped him.

Moving carefully, he placed the rifle on the table. The bowie knife, which had been left outside in order to free his hands, leaned against a log wall. He removed the gunbelt and laid it beside the rifle.

"Step away. Back up against the front wall."

He obeyed. The goggling eyes stared at the black well of the opening door. As he backed, he wiped sweat away from his forehead with the back of his right hand. When the hand moved back toward his side, he released the top button of his jacket.

"Hot," he mumbled. "Villows, you make me hot."

A man's body took shape in the opening.

"Anderson!" Hein said disgustedly. "I led myself be taken by *you!*"

Pale eyes like those of Willows hated him from a saturnine face. The railish man holding the shotgun looked as hard and pliant as a whiplash.

"Take a look at me, Dutchman. One-eye Anderson. A hundred dollars for an eye! Chicken feed to what you're gonna pay if you want to leave here alive."

Hein scratched his chest. "Vere iss Lotus?"

"What difference does it make? She won't go with you when you leave, if you leave. Maybe you won't see so good by then. I built a pen for you, Dutchman. I aim to lock you up and let you sweat."

Hein scratched himself again. When the hand came out, it held the shoulder gun. Before the victory-savoring Anderson could lift the shotgun,

Hein put two bullets into his chest. He let out a shriek of surprise and terror, in reaction triggering the cocked gun. The roaring blasts slammed into the floor and wall nowhere near Hein, for he was on the move. He kicked the legs from under the crumbling man. Glaring eyes threatened to burst from their sockets. He let out a cry of exultation. Anderson! Hein kicked him again, his boot thudding into unresisting flesh.

"Lotus!" he shouted. "Vere are you, Lotus?"

There was no answer from the dark beyond the open door.

Hein strode across to take up the bottle candle holder. He went through the door, holding the candle in order not to blind himself. The lone flicker provided only a frail contention with the dark. By it he made out the partial outlines of a great hollow in the cliff.

"Lotus?"

There was no movement, no answering voice.

From behind, a looped whip snapped down over his head. Held by strong hands, it hooked beneath his chin, tightening across his throat in front, hurting his larynx, strangling him as he was hauled backward into the log shelter.

He lost the candle bottle. The candle hit the floor and went out. Dropping the pistol, he clawed at the strangling whip as he sprawled backward on the floor. One flex of the whip was released. His assailant yanked it free. Hein flopped over on his face, thrusting with his muscular arms to propel himself to his feet. A flailing boot dislodged one arm. He went down again, rolled, and again tried to rise. Sensing another side-swing kick, he flailed an arm, and his assailant stepped away.

In a flash he was on his feet, hunching to attack.

A sharp warning. "Don't! I'll shoot out your lungs."

Hein disregarded the warning. He charged the shadowy form. It evaded him. Turning, he lunged toward the table to reclaim his holstered pistol and fell over the body on the floor. He had forgotten Pete Anderson.

"Cool down," the voice commanded. "Cool down, or you're dead."

A shot smashed through his fury. He was not hit, but the sound pierced the red whirlpool in his skull.

"Villows! It's you, Villows! *I kill you, too!*"

"Get up and go out where it is light. We've got some business to transact."

"Vere iss mine Lotus?"

"She is not your Lotus. She is my Lotus."

Hein had risen. "*Nein!*" he denied thickly. "She is Dean Dalke's *frau.*"

"That's not why you came after her."

"I take her back. I pay him vot he paid to me."

"I'll pay you nothing. Or Dalke. She is my property now. Part of our deal."

"No deal. Vere iss she?"

"*Outside.* I won't tell you again. You've got to learn to take orders. You count for nothing here."

Because Willows was slow to follow, Hein darted around to where he had left the bowie knife.

"Not there," Willows informed him tauntingly. "I watched you come in. We had you between us, me and Pete, just the way we planned."

Hein was looking with astonishment at the two whips in Willows' hands. Willows flung one of them at his feet.

"I'll fight you for the Chinese girl. Winner takes her. Then we'll settle what you pay us—me. Pay for two killings, Hein."

Hah! Anderson had a gun. *Schwein!*"

"The other one didn't have a gun. Did he, Hein? The other Dutchman?"

"I didt nod kill Gustave. You lie."

"Hogwash! Pick up your whip."

Hein complied. "You fight me zo?" he inquired suspiciously, licking his lips, the bulging eyes intent.

"I fight you zo. Pete said you took off your shirt. Go ahead."

"I leaf it on. You tagk off your gun."

"Sure, Mr. Hein. Excuse me while I put it inside where you can't grab it. Don't run away. I don't want to shoot you. I want to keep you barely alive to do some dickering. That is my brother in there on the floor. Pete Anderson. The man you blinded. My brother."

"You men scheme against me. You make big troubles."

"Your troubles have only begun. Pete built a pen for you inside your cave. You're going into it when I get you pared down to the bone, Mr. Hein. I don't know how you got the jump on old Pete. We had you trapped. You're a tricky gent. He should have known that. I watched you pick up the signs I left for you. I hurried ahead to signal Pete, then went back out so we would have you between us. It was slick the way he baited you with the Chinese girl. Poor old Pete. Sometimes he was too careless. It was on account of him we got nabbed and slapped into the pen. Do you think I'm careless, Mr. Hein? Fighting you with a whip?"

"Vere is Lotus?"

"Probably shut up in Pete's pen for safekeeping. She don't know Pete used her for bait. Or maybe she does by now. She is smart, too smart to answer when you hollered. Looks like she would rather stay in our pen than go home with you."

"*Schwein!*" Hein popped the lash.

"You think you're a past master with the whip. I've been practicing up for you, Mr. Hein. You're fighting both me and Pete."

He shook out the whip. Hein did not wait. A curling lash flicked out. Willows barely avoided the strike at his eyes.

"Sneaky, eh? I'm gonna strip you to your bones."

He sent the wicked lash at Hein, who fended with his left arm and struck in return, an underhanded snap that cracked within inches of the surprised Willows' face. It should have reached him. When it did not, Hein discovered that the whip Willows had thrown to him had a shorter lash. Seconds later a bite into the flesh of his forearm and a ripped sleeve apprised him of another imbalance. Willows' lash was tipped with a thin strip of sharp metal. Willows had staged an unequal fight.

Muttering blistering curses, Hein shielded his face from another strike. Again the metal knifed the protecting arm. Willows had not boasted. He was skilful with the whip. Determined to maim.

Hein looked for the bowie knife. His quick side glances searched the shed, hoping to see an axe. Apparently there was nothing. . . .

Razor-sharp metal sliced along his jaw, a fine-line streak. He tried to move closer. Willows glided away like a dancer, the thin, wide mouth twisted in a derisive grin.

Suddenly Hein rushed, a flurry of flashing strikes, over, under, from the side. In retreat for the first time, Willows seemed dismayed by the skill of the furious man he had insultingly dubbed past master. The hard features lost their smile. Blood laced the whip hand which flicked the metal-tipped lash. Disregarding punishment, Hein bulled in. The sleeve on his left arm now was tattered and stained with blood.

Below the injured jaw his neck was stickily red. Bulging eyes blazed with consummate hate. He curled the whip into a club, boring in to flail, chop, slash—a whirlwind of inescapable violence.

At close quarters Willows was unable to use the lash. For the moment unmindful of his position, he found himself bulled into the shed. He clubbed his own whip. They stood face to face, clubbing at each other. For the moment neither seemed to care how much he suffered in the savage desire to hurt the other, to smash, to kill. Words poured from Hein as he fought.

"I didt not kill Gustave. Dummkopf ideas he had. Foolishments. Always played jokes. Spoilt. Too much monies. Order me find man. I find Anderson, yess— I do it for Gustave. Uncle Wilhelm visit us. Excitement, hah! Plays jokes on Uncle Wilhelm. Shows him Wild West. Gustave fix op like Indian. Feathers, hah! Holler, dance around, run in house. Uncle Wilhelm old soldier. Kill Gustave with axe. Think he Indian. I not there. I at the sheds. Ve not haff barn yet."

Hein had not slain the other Dutchman. The Anderson brothers had nothing on him at all. Willows no longer tried to retreat. His plot had been blown apart. Kill or be killed. It had come down to that.

The rush of words did not cease. Hein emptied the vitriol of the years. Uncle Wilhelm had been frantic when he had discovered his horrible deed.

He had run down to tell Hein, begged him to keep the terrible news from Faith. The property was in Uncle Wilhelm's name. He kept limits on the spending of his prodigal son. "Tagk care of Faith. Yeah, I tagk care of Faith. He promise send me papers. He don' keep his vort. He send papers, yess, ven I marry Faith. Papers in both our names. Faith, she own mit me. Uncle Wilhelm not keep his vort. . . .

Hein's nose had been smashed. His lips were a bloody pulp. Reddened eyes swam in flaming sockets. His cap was gone, his jacket ripped to tatters, the doeskin pants forever ruined. Patches of lingering polish on his boots shone through grime and scratchings. Torn skin dangled from his whip hand. As Willows weakened, Hein forsook the clubbing attack and backed away. Standing off, he cut Willows into complete submission, the master at his best, or worst. Willows collapsed upon his knees. Bleeding hands tried to protect his face. Hein lashed them to bloody pulps.

"You can have her," Willows gasped. "You win. You win."

He flattened on the ground, face down, head hidden in protective arms. Grunting, spitting blood, Hein curled the whip again, the weighted handle extended from a bloody, tight-fisted hand. On weaving legs he moved toward his prostrate foe. Bending unbalanced him. Bracing. he lifted the weighted whip to crush Willows' skull.

"Lay off, Hein!" someone shouted. "That's enough!"

The shout penetrated his leaden resolve. He caught himself, having nearly fallen again. Turning with a great effort, he saw as through a red haze what seemed to be a shimmering host of men lining the open front of the shed. They wavered to and from each other, blending, separating. He recognized none, did not accept their presence, thought he was out of his head. A figure moved toward him. It shrank and distended, shrank and distended. He did not resist as Sudbury Pinkham took the whip from his hand.

"Gawd! What an awful sight!"

The words meant nothing to Hein. Swollen eyelids sluggishly curtained the staring eyes. The bloody, filthy features seemed to squeeze together. He fell on top of Willows, who writhed and crawled away.

"Tend to them," Pinkham said to Bart Kinney.

He strode through the door of the log shelter, calling Lotus' name. "Sudbury Pinkham here. Lotus, do you hear me?"

A faint cry came to him from the dark beyond the open inner door. He nearly stumbled over Anderson's body, moved around it, went on into deeper darkness. His voice became a roar. "Lotus, where are you?"

"Back here! I'm locked in. There are candles in a box behind the stove."

Candles! No coal oil in these wilds.

He was lighting a candle when Joe Enright hobbled in from the shed. When Enright saw the body, he inquired, "Crawlin' crawdads, who is that?"

Pinkham handed him the candle, lit another for himself. "Never saw him before. Lotus is back in that dark hole. Locked in, she says. I'm going to skin Willows alive for this."

Enright stooped to examine the body. "Somebody put two shots into his brisket. He is still hanging onto his shotgun. It has been fired."

He followed Pinkham through the door. Their candles dispelled the darkness as they advanced. The cave was shallow. At the rear a stockade-like structure had been contstructed from rock floor to rock overhead. Beyond spaced gaps between upright posts, something moved.

Pinkham swore. "Lotus, Lotus, what have they done to you?"

Her voice sang with joy. "Hush, Sudbury. Being shut up hasn't hurt me. They built this cage for Mr. Hein. I wasn't afraid of Will. The other one frightened me. He was so full of hate."

"I wouldn't say Willows was free of it."

"Who was the fellow?" Enright asked. "I suppose Hein killed him?"

"They were brothers. Will's real name is Anderson. They had a grudge against Mr. Hein. Oh, Sudbury, they were planning to get money out of Mr. Dalke, sell me back to him. Set me free, set me free."

Pinkham had examined the gate. The pen was sturdy enough to hold a bull. "It is fastened with a padlock and chain," he said angrily. "I suppose the key is in Willows' pocket. Stay with her, Joe. At least you can give her light." He handed his candle to Enright.

When he went outside, he saw Fritz Hein stretched out in front of the shed. Two of the men were taking off his shredded clothing. Willows still lay in the shed. He had turned upon his back. A red hand lay across his forehead.

About to search him for the key, Pinkham caught sight of an axe hanging on pegs high on the log end of the shelter. He took it down and strode back to the cage. Enright and the girl had been talking.

"She is fine, Pink. Stop fretting. It's all over but the shouting."

"Who wants to shout? All she has had is trouble, trouble, trouble. Treated like a dumb animal. You'd think she would hate everyone."

"Seems like you're doing it for her," Enright observed.

Pinkham savagely attacked the posts circled by the chain, venting his anger on the confining wood, smashing away Lotus' cage. When the barrier hung in ruins, the girl thrust it open and came out. She hesitated, looking at Pinkham, then ran into his arms.

Enright stuck one of the candles on a splinter and

went out of the cave, leaving them alone. The man he loved like a brother, and the woman Pinkham loved. The wife of another man. She had referred to her husband as *Mr.* Dalke!

Trouble. It wasn't *all over*. Enright was well aware of that.

He placed the candle in a tin cup and gathered up the array of weapons to carry them outside. "Have someone look after this artillery," he called to Kinney, who was with the men attending to Hein. One of them had brought water from the brook in a wooden bucket. Hein was washing himself. His movements were lethargic. He was not talking.

Kinney stayed where he was. He ordered Pruitt to take charge of the weapons.

Willows was sitting up. No one bothered with him. "You're a first-class stinker, Willows," Enright said to him, "keeping that girl in a pen. Looks like things didn't pan out for you and that ugly gink inside."

Willows did not speak. He sat, head bowed, chin on his chest. Under lowered brows, the shielded eyes watched the group around Fritz Hein.

"Partners, hey?" Enright guessed, undeterred by silence. "What do you have here, an old outlaw set-up? The more I know about you, the more I believe Dalke was right about you. I think you did shoot some feller in the back. Lotus said you didn't bother her. That's one thing in your favor, though

I think you would have got around to it."

He turned as Lotus and Pinkham came out of the shelter. Lotus looked radiant. Pinkham was grinning like a school kid turned loose in a candy shop. She walked demurely at his side. They were not touching, but one familiar with the language of love would know their hearts were embracing.

Willows lifted his head to look at them. The girl's eyes widened when they noticed his condition, but she passed him as if he were not there. Pinkham saw the group around Hein and steered her to the front of the shelter.

The sight of Lotus stirred the crew. Someone cried, "Hooray!" They left Hein to come to her, clustering about, eagerly questioning. Even Gabe Kinney came. No one saw Willows rise to his feet. He was indeed a horrible sight, but he moved with something of the habitual litheness. Stepping over to the ricked wood, he thrust a bloody hand into an opening and withdrew Hein's bowie knife.

Willows ran, ran with surprising ability for one who had seemed so helpless. He broke into the open, seeming to gain speed as he moved. His glance was fixed on the man seated on the ground.

Left alone for the moment, Hein methodically, even doggedly continued to wash away blood and grime. He was naked to the waist. His boots had been removed. He heard the outbreak of shouting, heard the girl scream, and at the last heard the running feet. He turned to look just as the bowie knife swung downward at his unprotected neck. The deadly knife almost severed his head from his body.

Willows ran on, his burst of destructive energy swiftly spent. He drove reluctant flesh, reaching for whatever resources his body held in store, weaving, dodging about, expending already depleted strength, running toward the upper valley away from his foes into a refuge he knew and they did not.

Among the men were those who had witnessed the killing, too stunned by the quick deed for instant reaction. Pistols appeared in clutching hands. Too closely grouped to shoot, they spread for room. It was Gabe Kinney who kept his cool.

Lotus hid her face against Pinkham, rendering him powerless to do anything about Willows.

Kinney took up Hein's rifle from the small pile of weapons guarded by Pruitt. He looked at the action, released the safety and flopped on the ground, his left elbow stanchioned for a rest. Unhurriedly he took aim, unruffled by the yammering pistols. He squeezed the trigger. The running man leaped into the air like a rabbit struck in flight. Arms outflung, he plunged ahead to crash sprawling upon the earth.

The pistols were silent. Kinney arose somewhat lamely. His glance remained on the silent figure up the slanting valley. It did not move.

Awed men looked at each other. They looked at Kinney. They looked at Lotus Flower huddled on the ground beside the log wall, her face hidden in her hands.

No one said anything. No one felt like talking.

Pinkham knelt beside Lotus and took her in his arms.

Two days later they stopped at the cow camp. The Anderson brothers lay buried side by side in their mountain hideaway. Aside from saddle gear which was needed, their personal possessions had been left behind, but the animals had been brought out. No one wanted to leave them to the creatures of the wild. Willows' appaloosa had been found outside the defile, saddled, tethered to a tree.

Foreman Kinney, his employer dead, had wondered what to do.

"You're the big cheese now," Pinkham told him. "Keep on doing what you've been doing until we learn the ropes. Joe and I will get the lowdown from Judge Toomey when we get back to town. I don't know what will happen to the property. Do you know whether Hein made a will?"

The foreman shook his head. Looking thoughtful, he delved into a saddle pocket and brought out a small roll of canvas tied with string. Unrolling it, he took out a square of paper, which he handed to Lotus.

"Maybe this will help, if you can read Dutch. This is what brought the old lady up here to the camp.

Wanted us to watch her sign, then put our names to it."

Lotus looked at the paper, puzzled over it for a moment, then shook her head. She handed it to Pinkham. Unable to decipher the script, he looked at the signatures. He could make out the date. August 7, 1897.

"We saw Mrs. Hein sign this paper.   Faith Hein
Gabe Kinney
Bert Parker
Thor Jansson
Carl Brown
Fred Harris, his mark X
Jim Smith, his mark X
Pete Sims, his mark X
Louis Scioto, his mark X
Hans Werner, his mark X"

"I think it is a will," Pinkham said to Lotus. "She wrote something about having money for you."

"That's what I think, too," Kinney agreed. "She told me to keep it and give it to nobody but Lotus. Made me promise. Poor old lady. I didn't realize she was so far gone."

Lotus was in tears. "Oh, Sudbury, when you told me about her dying all alone—poor, poor soul! I came to her too late."

The extra livestock had joined the herds on the

benchland. Kinney had decided that Pruitt should go along with him to the ranch, probably to remain and look after the property. Lotus was riding Dean Dalke's black horse.

When the five rode down out of the foothills to the ranch, the first change noted was a small, newly fenced area south of the cottonwoods. In the center of the enclosure a board cross surmounted a mound of earth. The arms of the cross bore a name freshly painted in black: "BERT."

Thor Jansson came out as they approached the house. He was carrying a shotgun. The long narrow face wore a smile. He was glad to see them.

"So you're still on the job," the foreman said good-humoredly. "I'm glad to see you, Swede. We need you. The boss is dead. So is the old lady. It's gonna take all hands to see this thing through."

Jansson stood for a long moment assimilating the information. The blue eyes studied their faces. Enright thought he looked about ready to cry.

"I take care of Bert. Find house blowed up. I stay to watch over safe."

"Where is it—" Pinkham inquired— "this safe you have been nursing?"

Jansson went into the arsenal, where he pointed out a large brass key hanging by a small chain from a notch in a gun rack.

"Yeah, but where is the safe?" Enright asked. "There is none here."

"In kitchen. I know that a long time. Mr. Hein don' believe in banks. Keeps money at ranch. Safe is lower part of one cabinet in the kitchen. Bolted to the floor. He keep key locked up in here."

Enright looked hard at him. "Behold an honest man. Jansson, I'm thankful you didn't go back to Sweden. We need more folks we can trust."

Jansson showed puzzlement. "Sweden? I born in Philadelphia."

He didn't know why they laughed, but after a moment he joined them.

They learned the particulars of the tragedy at the ranch on the following day. The county sheriff arrived in company with Judge Toomey and a newly appointed deputy. Sid Durham had died before the posse reached home base. A damaged artery, undetected by his attendants, had ruptured while he rode unconscious in the surrey. Tillie Haworth had left for parts unknown. No one seemed to care.

When Lotus heard that she had been widowed and would share in Dalke's property, she shut herself away in Faith Hein's room, overwhelmed by her new estate, horrified by the manner of Dalke's dying, torn by emotions she had never experienced before. Serenity gone, she gave way to shock. She grieved for Faith Hein, even found she could grieve for the others who had been slain.

"Let her alone for a while," Enright said to his worried friend. "Give her plenty of time."

Time. There is an old saying that love will find a way.

Judge Toomey knew enough about German script to interpret Faith's writing.

"Crawlin' crawdads," Joe Enright breathed in awe. "Lotus will get the whole shebang!"

So it happened that the Chinese girl who had wanted nothing but love was given everything, even her heart's desire.